A WANTON WOMAN

MAIL ORDER BRIDE OF SLATE SPRINGS - BOOK 1

VANESSA VALE

Copyright © 2016 by Vanessa Vale

This is a work of fiction. Names, characters, places and incidents are the products of the author's imagination and used fictitiously. Any resemblance to actual persons, living or dead, businesses, companies, events or locales is entirely coincidental.

All rights reserved.

No part of this book may be reproduced in any form or by any electronic or mechanical means, including information storage and retrieval systems, without written permission from the author, except for the use of brief quotations in a book review.

Cover design: Bridger Media

Cover graphic: Hot Damn Stock

TOWN NOTICE:

Passed by unanimous vote of the town council, September 16, 1885, law 642. The Marriage Law. Because of deficient numbers of women in the area, it is now legal within the city of Slate Springs, Colorado and the surrounding areas, for two or more men to legally wed one woman. All ceremonies will be performed by the Justice of the Peace and will be considered valid and legally binding until death upon the bride or both/all husbands.

Signed,
  Luke Tate
  Town Mayor

1

elia
 Tyler, Texas
September 1885

It was too hot to be outside. Although, it was too hot to be indoors as well. The summer heat had yet to diminish and the ground was hard packed and bone dry. I glanced up and squinted. There wasn't a cloud in the sky. No way to shield myself—besides my straw hat—from the sun. My dress, with the high neck and long sleeves, was stifling. Sweat soaked the back of my corset and I longed to strip off the excess layers of clothing for just my shift.

It had been a long day. John's office hours were in the mornings on Tuesdays and he'd had several patients waiting when we arrived at eight. My husband wasn't the only doctor in town, but people came long distances if ailing enough and there was enough business for all three of them. Today's ailments had included an impacted tooth, a colicky infant, a case of pneumonia and a broken finger. When he left for lunch, I was left behind to clean up and send those who arrived after the noon hour—when John went to the hotel's restaurant to eat his meal—in the direction of the other two doctors. He was very precise, very strict in his routine and did not vary from it.

While he spent his afternoon at his home office—always with the door closed so as not to be disturbed—I often went to the houses of those who had been seen, checking on them, tending to them. Specifically, the women patients. None of the men, for it would not be appropriate. I wasn't even *supposed* to visit the ladies, but who else would? Not John, for if they did not appear in his office, injury apparent, or have money to pay for a house call, he was not interested.

And so I spent my afternoon tending to the sick, rocking babies, even washing a few dishes. John laughed at my *pedestrian* afternoon activity, always telling me I was lowering myself to such tedium. But was I supposed to sit home and read and needlepoint? I could not support such a stagnant life.

And so that was why I stood in Mrs. Borden's kitchen, scrubbing a pot. I blew a wayward curl off my face, but it clung to the sweat on my brow. Just delivering her third child, she was in bed recovering with two young ones climbing over her and the newborn while her husband went to work in the cotton fields.

As I moved on to clean the previous night's dinner dishes, she called from the bedroom. "It will be your turn soon and I will come and help you."

I paused in my scrubbing and looked down at my flat stomach. No, there would be no turn for me. No children; John was a very independent sort, and expected me to be as well. I knew when I married him that he wanted a helpmeet, not a coddler. I'd been well and fine with that, for I'd been raised by stern parents who did not dote. I knew no other way. I would have been unaccustomed to a man who hugged and lavished me with affection.

But in the past five years, I'd grown to change my mind. Watching other couples who were blatantly in love —like the Bordens—proved that I had missed something, and would never see it in my own union. Without children to tend, my life was empty. *I* was empty. To John, I was officially barren. Officially not a true wife, for I could not fulfill the one duty that he could not accomplish on his own.

And so, forlorn and overheated, I returned home, forgoing any other afternoon visits. Closing the front door behind me, I noticed that John's office door was open. Odd, for he never appeared before five. As I removed my hat and placed it on the table beside the door, I heard voices from upstairs. Murmuring, then a sigh. A woman's cry.

I glanced up as if I could see through the ceiling. I

knew what it was. *Who* it was. At least I knew it was John and a woman. A rhythmic thumping followed. They were fucking. In my bed. John barely touched me, so I knew he took his needs to someone else. A brothel or a widow, someone who he felt worthy of his desires. But he'd never slaked these needs in our own home. While I doubted he loved me, he respected me enough to keep his women separate from me. Until now.

"Yes! Right there. *Harder*."

My eyes widened at the carnality of the woman's words, the desperate tone. While angry he would flaunt his behavior in such a way, I was also curious. Curious as to what John did to make her so satisfied. I'd *never* cried out like that before. Ever.

I tiptoed up the stairs, careful to avoid the creaky fourth step. The bedroom door was closed, so I slipped into the other bedroom that had an adjoining door. Meant for a nursery, it sat unused. But I knew the door was open about a foot to allow for air to circulate and could easily watch. And that was where I stood, behind the connecting door, and observed my husband in bed with a woman. I did not recognize her, for her pale hair was unbound and covered her face. She was also naked, on her hands and knees with her wrists restrained and tied to the metal scrollwork of the headboard with *my* dressing gown tie. The garment itself lay forgotten on the floor beside the heap of their discarded clothing.

John was behind her, naked too, and fucking her. His hands gripped her hips as he took her forcefully, the sound of his hips slapping against her upturned bottom filled the air.

"Is that hard enough?" he growled, the muscles in his neck corded and tense.

She tossed her head and her grip turned white on the bed rails. Her breasts, which were very large, swung with each thrust. It was carnal and dark and decadent and I'd never seen John like this. He was lost to desire, lost to the power he had over the woman. Never so... overcome by his baser needs. Whenever he took me, he was quiet and passive, his hips shifting enough for his cock to move in and out for him to release his seed.

He smacked her bottom, the crack of it making her cry out. She groaned, but it was not in pain. "You're such a slut, letting me take you like this. You need it, don't you? Your husband thinks it's hysteria that makes you a frustrated wife, but you're just a whore that needs a big cock."

"Yes!" she cried again. This was what I was supposed to look like while being fucked? Wild and wanton and in the throes of pleasure so intense I loved having my bottom smacked?

I'd never heard him speak in such a way before, his words so blunt and cruel. His voice was rough-edged, not the flat, even tone to which I was accustomed. He'd never spoken to me in such a fashion, never gripped me with such intent, never *fucked* me that way either. I hadn't even known you could.

But I was not like this woman. Her figure was unlike

mine. She was tall and lean, with a very ample bosom and a small behind. I was petite and curvy, round hips and bottom and yet my breasts were much smaller. Had he chosen her to fuck because she was the antithesis of me? Did her appearance bring about this change in him? Was I that lacking? I had to assume the answer was yes.

John only took me at night when it was dark, the soft light of the lantern beside the bed casting a soft glow to the room. There was no talking. He just pressed me onto my back, worked my nightgown up as he spread my legs and pushed inside me without any preamble. He did breathe hard, but only when he spent his seed, the exertion from it mild in comparison to the vigor he applied now. He never perspired, never groaned. When done, he'd tug my nightgown back down, pull the covers over me and roll over onto his side to sleep. I would be sore and unfulfilled, seed sticky on my thighs and the bed beneath me.

This woman, she was not unfulfilled. The way she shifted and circled her hips, the way her skin glowed with a sheen of perspiration, the way she was panting and chanting *yes, yes, yes* over and over again, it was quite obvious that she was enjoying herself. I'd never *enjoyed* myself with John, never felt the same abandon, the obvious desire this woman did at my husband's hands, or cock. The way she moaned her release, her body tensing even as John continued to pound into her, I knew now I'd never come before.

I was more upset at being cheated of this kind of deep

and dark—and pleasurable—connection between two people than the fact that my husband was sharing it with someone else. I'd known of his philandering for some time, but not who he did it with, or where. I'd certainly not expected *this*.

I wanted this. I wanted someone to tangle their fingers in my hair and yank my head back. I wanted someone to take me hard from behind. I wanted a man's handprint to be a bright pink on my bottom. I wanted passion.

The front door slammed, which made me jump.

"Marie!" A man's voice bellowed from below.

John's motions stilled, his cock deep inside the woman as she whipped her head toward the door. Her eyes widened in surprise and panic.

"It's my husband!" she hissed, but couldn't move, tied as she was to the bed and John behind her.

The man came up the steps, his heavy tread sounding as if he took them two at a time. The bedroom door swung so hard it slammed into the wall. I jumped and gasped, then bit my lip. A big man stood in the doorway. Dressed in a suit and tie, his hair was slicked back with sweat, beads of it dripping down his temples. He was breathing hard, as if he'd run all the way across town. He wasn't a farmer or a laborer, but a well-to-do man. The cut of his clothes was telling, and John wouldn't have taken a low-class mistress. But a married one? This man was scorned. The gun in his hands proved that and I bit my lip again to stifle the panic that wanted to slip out.

Proved that he was a little insane, too. Mad with jealousy? I felt ridiculed and ashamed at being tossed aside. I could only imagine this man's rage at being discovered a cuckold.

John pulled out of the woman—Marie—and turned on his knees toward the other man. His cock was red and swollen and shiny with the woman's arousal. Marie was trapped by her wrists being tied, but she tipped onto her side and pulled her knees up to try to hide. She was like a child who covered their eyes and thought they could not be seen. Her motions did nothing to hide her nakedness or the view of her used pussy. Her crime, and John's, was indisputable.

"Neil," she cried, her eyes widening. John put his hands up as if to ward the man off, but he said nothing. What was there to say?

Neil narrowed his eyes as his chest heaved. There was no hesitation, no deliberation. He shot John square in the chest.

The sound reverberated in the room and I covered my mouth with my hand to cover my cry of surprise. Blood bloomed on his chest and John put his hands over the hole. He only looked down at the wound before he fell to his side, dead. I was not the doctor, but I knew a shot to the heart would make death instantaneous. Marie screamed and pleaded with her husband as she shuffled up onto her knees and tugged at the bonds that held her trapped. Instead of a playful game of bondage, it kept her right where Neil wanted her when he shot her, too. Once, then twice.

I barely breathed, my ears ringing from the report of the gun. I didn't dare move a muscle, afraid he'd see me and come after me next. Neil stood and looked at the bodies for a few seconds. Maybe a minute. I had no idea of time. I just remained as still as possible behind the door, hoping he couldn't hear the frantic beat of my heart. Surely, he'd shoot me too if I was discovered. While he had reason for his actions, it was still cold-blooded murder. He took a deep breath, then another, then spun on his heels, stomped down the steps and out the door. The quiet left in his wake was just as deafening as the gunshots.

My legs quivered, then folded. I slid down the wall to the floor, a crumpled, wilted heap. My hands shook and I tried to keep myself calm, to keep the excess energy from overwhelming me. That was where the sheriff and my neighbors found me a few minutes later, the dirty secrets of my marriage no longer hidden. Instead, they were naked and dead in my own bed.

2

*L*uke
Denver, Colorado
December 1885

"You didn't have to do this," Walker murmured, standing with me on the train platform as the westbound train pulled in. It was loud, hissing and clunking as it came to a stop. Finally. Two hours behind schedule and in that time I should have turned around and left. But a woman waited, a woman who was my bride and I could not be cruel to her. It was not her fault I'd been proxy married to a stranger. The blame fell solely on me.

"I do," I replied, my breath coming out in a big white cloud. The sun had slid behind the mountains and night was falling fast, the temperature dropping well below freezing. Any snow that had melted earlier in the day was now turning to ice on the brick walkways.

Tucking the collar of my coat up about my neck, I looked down the length of the train, knowing she would soon appear. My bride. My *mail order* bride. A stranger with a piece of paper that tied us in legal matrimony. What would she look like? Tall or short? Homely or beautiful? It mattered not. What did matter was that I was the first to marry under the new law of Slate Springs. I glanced at Walker, stalwart and quiet beside me. "Are you having second thoughts? Is that the problem?"

"Fuck, Luke, I said I'd do it and I keep my word." His dark eyes flared in anger, but it was quickly banked.

I sighed. "Shit, sorry. I'm just... this is just not how I expected it."

"What? Freezing our balls off for a woman we're committed to for the rest of our lives just because Slate Springs doesn't have enough women?"

Yeah, that described it pretty well.

"Fine, I did this out of duty, but really, I want someone to share my life with, just like most men in town. Children. Companionship. Hell, someone to warm my bed on a night like tonight."

I tugged the collar of my coat up against the wind that whipped down the platform.

"All you had to do was come down the mountain. Denver has enough women who would gladly marry the mayor of Slate Springs, and a mine owner to boot." He lifted his hands and cupped them around his mouth, exhaled warm air onto them.

The Trusty mine was putting out silver at a pace that was making me as rich as those up in Butte digging up copper. I knew it wouldn't last, that the vein would dry up eventually, but I had more money than I needed in my lifetime. Now, it was time to share it with others, like a wife and children.

"I'm more than a mine owner. I don't want a woman who's only interested in my money. I want a woman who wants *me*."

Standing still, the cold seeped through the bottom of my boots. Passengers began to alight the train. Porters passed us to help the weary travelers with their baggage.

I turned to my brother, trying to justify this marriage. "I took the job just to keep Thomkins from getting the position. If I remember, we flipped for the job."

The corner of his mouth tipped up. "Yeah, and you lost. Being mayor might keep Thomkins from fucking up the town, but it gets you a bride, too."

Yes, being mayor and voting on the law that allows two men to marry one woman had me setting the example, a precedence for other men in town to follow. Thus, Walker and I were in Denver meeting a woman who would be ours. Maybe I should have let Thomkins be mayor after all. He didn't need to find a bride. He'd been married to the meek Agnes Thomkins for ten years or so. He'd been an asshole pretty much since birth when his daddy founded the town and he'd been one ever since. He wouldn't do right by the town if he were mayor, probably ban mining or some such nonsense when there were mouths to feed. My anger toward Thomkins was enough to keep me in the leadership role and keep me standing in the cold waiting for our mail order bride.

"And you," I added. "You get a bride because of how much we fucking hate Thomkins, too." We were in this together. This woman would be ours together.

I heard him sigh, but he said nothing more.

Passengers began to pass and I watched them all closely, looking for Celia Lawrence, widow from Tyler, Texas. And my bride. Celia Tate, now. I had no knowledge of her appearance, only that she was a widow and twenty-five years old. I gripped the Bible in my hand and placed it so it could better seen. While I was not an overly pious man—I was committing to marry a woman in a very unbiblical way, with Walker and without our union blessed in a church—but the Bible was the way for Mrs. Lawrence to discern me from the crowd.

"Are *you* sure?" I asked, wanting to confirm one last time. "You vowed never to marry again after Ruth's death. You can still change your mind. I can find someone else."

He could back out, but I couldn't. The proxy marriage was legally binding. Luke Tate, husband. Celia Lawrence, wife. But I had no interest in sharing a bride with just any man. I'd only do it with my brother. We were close, close enough to have shared women in the past, to have the same interests—and darker desires—when it came to taking a woman. Some might find our predilections to be sinful or even wrong, but dominating a woman only led to her pleasure, her ultimate satisfaction. We put her first. Sure, we might tie her up and spank her ass, even fuck it, too, but she'd like it. No, she'd *love* it.

"I want children, too," he admitted. "But love?" Shrugging his shoulders, I knew he was jaded. "That's for you. She deserves it and you'll give it to her. This works perfectly for me."

I angled my head toward the emptying train.

Walker shrugged. "We have to hope."

The bulk of the passengers had left the platform and had moved quickly into the warm station. Only a few years old, it was an impressive structure, a sign that Denver was booming. I didn't care for the city. Too many people, too much noise. The only reason I was here was for—

Her.

She was walking toward us, eyeing the Bible. I should have approached her, asked her name and grabbed the small bag she held. But I couldn't. I just stared. And stared as if my feet had frozen to the ground.

"Fuck." I heard Walker mumble under his breath as he took her in as well. It seemed my brother had the same intense—and instant—attraction for her. "Look at her," he whispered.

Yes, we were truly fucked, for Mrs. Celia Lawrence was everything I could have imagined in a bride. Petite, her curves couldn't be hidden beneath her light jacket. Her pale hair was up and tucked beneath a prim hat. The

A Wanton Woman

lanterns that lit the platform from the dusk set her skin to a warm gold. Her cheeks were flushed from the cold and I could see that her pale eyes were wary and hopeful at the same time. She stilled when she shifted her gaze away from the Bible and onto me, but she tilted up her chin and took another step closer.

She was... fuck, incredible. Lovely. Dainty. Shy. Daring. I wanted her. Instantly and desperately. My cock hardened and I was thankful my coat hid the reaction. She was my bride.

She was mine. Mine!

Walker had his wits about him, unlike me, for he moved around me to approach her. "Mrs. Lawrence?" he asked.

She looked up at him, a frown forming in her brow. "Yes. Mr. Tate?"

Her soft voice had me moving. Finally. I was fucking it all up and I hadn't even said a word. She was just too... perfect and I felt as if I'd been hit on the head with a support beam from the mine. I cleared my throat and joined the two, removing my hat. "I'm Luke Tate, ma'am."

She glanced at the Bible once more, then up at my face. Way up. I was so much taller; she only came up to my shoulder. She offered me a small smile, but I could tell it took effort. I was a big man, and a stranger at that. She was very brave to travel so far on her own, to be wed to a complete stranger. No, two strangers. I'd just met her and I was very proud of her. I wanted to take away the wariness and replace it with... hell, what would she look like when I made her come the first time? I'd find out soon enough if my cock had any say.

"It is... nice to meet you. Please, call me Celia." Her voice was deep and sultry, a complete surprise and made my cock hard.

A shiver shook her small frame.

"Where is your coat?" I asked. Pushing the Bible into Walker's chest, I stripped off mine and wrapped it about her shoulders.

Her tongue darted out to lick her bottom lip and I was transfixed. "I don't have one. It is not this cold in Texas."

Her voice had a slight accent to it, a slight twang that spoke of how far she'd traveled.

The cold air hit my torso and I could only imagine how chilled she'd been.

Smiling, she held the oversized garment together at the front. It was so large that it hung down to past her knees. It would keep her warm in the short term.

"Didn't Mrs. Carstairs from the agency tell you your destination was Colorado?" The woman at the mail order bride service should have advised her of something as simple as winter wardrobe.

She lifted her shoulders and almost snuggled into the garment. "Yes, of course. But no shops in Tyler have coats like this. It is too warm year-round for such items in Texas." She glanced about and took in the snow that had been shoveled into piles to clear the platform. "I have never even seen snow before."

I looked at the old snow, crusty hard from the top

being melted by the sun and then frozen at night, gray from the soot and ash from the trains. This patch was far from remarkable. When we were home, she would know snow. Perhaps even become quite sick of it before the season ended.

"Come, let's get out of the cold then," Walker said.

Realizing I had yet to introduce her to her other husband, I felt even more of a bumbling fool. "May I present my brother, Walker?"

She didn't know he was also her husband and the train platform was not where I wanted to enlighten her. The last thing I wanted to do was scare her right back on the train. No fucking way. She was here, she was mine and I was not letting her go.

With his hands full, he did not remove his hat, only tipped it with his fingers as he held the Bible. "Ma'am."

We turned toward the station, working our way down the long platform. At an icy spot, I took her elbow and guided her around. "Careful," I warned.

If she had never seen snow, I had to doubt she'd encountered ice before. I did not need my bride breaking something within five minutes of her arrival. I could barely feel her through the thickness of my coat, but I had my hand on her and that was a start.

Once inside the warm station, I stopped. Walker stood to her side so that we blocked out the noise and crowds behind us. "Are you hungry?" I asked.

"Tired?" Walker added.

She laughed then, deep and throaty, as she looked

between the two of us. "I am not used to such attentions. From one man, let alone two."

She would get used to it soon enough, but not here. Union Station was not where I wanted to show her my attentions, or that she'd be getting them from Walker, too. When she learned she was married to both of us, I didn't know how she would react, although I had to assume with great surprise. While being married to two men was legal in Slate Springs, it was not elsewhere. Especially in a large town like Denver.

Glancing between us, she replied, "I am both."

Both? Oh yes, hungry and tired.

Nodding, I looked her over from her stylish hat to her spun gold hair, her lovely oval face, full lips, flushed cheeks. My coat hid her fashionable dress, but it had been crisp and fresh, even after her journey, her hair neat. She was concerned for her appearance, but did not seem vain. "We will return to the hotel then where you may rest and eat."

"Your town is too far to travel to now?"

Walker looked up at the large clock on the wall above the ticket counter. Five-fifteen. "Slate Springs is in the mountains, over a day's ride from here. The weather is good so the pass remains open, but we expect it to be snowed in before the new year. We do not need to push ourselves to return tonight, for while it is clear, it is very dark. As you said, you do not have the proper clothing. Tomorrow is soon enough."

Yes, I wasn't spending the first night with her—it

couldn't be called a wedding night as we were already proxy married—on the back of a horse. I wanted her on her back and me over her. "We have a room at a hotel down the street," I added, shifting because I had to hide my hard cock.

"Pass?" she asked as she looked behind her one last time before we led her out of the station to the busy street. Horses and wagons filled the thoroughfare.

I tucked my hat back onto my head. While the air was frigid, it did nothing to cool my ardor. Nothing would, not until I was buried deep inside her and filling her with my seed. Even then, I'd want her again. I was absolutely sure of that.

3

uke

"The road to Slate Springs follows a canyon up into the mountains to the west of here. It goes so high that it is snowed in for the winter. Denver is on this side of the pass, our town on the other."

She slowed her pace but did not stop walking as we continued down the sidewalk toward our hotel. "You mean we will be isolated?"

I glanced at Walker, but could not tell his expression with it being dark and his face in shadow beneath the brim of his hat. Many people had difficulties being in a town that was cut off from the rest of the world. The snow and cold was sometimes too much for people to handle. By the time spring thaw came, many men had turned slightly insane. Thus, the new law. If the men had their beds warmed and a family to care for, they might find the long winters much easier to pass.

"That's right," Walker said. While Celia couldn't tell his words were guarded, as his brother, I could hear it plain as day. "Once the snow comes in earnest, the town is cut off until spring."

"What if it had been snowed in earlier than usual? Would I have been stuck here in Denver while you, Mr. Tate, remained on the other side of the pass?"

Her question was unexpected. I feared she would be concerned about being trapped in a small town with us, not trapped without us. I stopped on the sidewalk, tilted her chin up with my fingers. Her skin was soft, like silk, yet chilled from the cold. Her eyes met mine. "Luke. Call me Luke. We would never leave you alone like that," I replied, my voice gentle. "We have been in Denver three days waiting for you, considering just such an occurrence."

Her eyes widened. "You... you have?"

It was the surprise in her voice that kept me from responding, for I knew there was much to learn about her from that alone.

"We've been waiting for you, Celia," I told her. All my life. I just didn't know it.

"Let's get out of the cold."

I glanced at Walker as we turned toward the hotel

once more. Neither of us would leave our bride alone in a big city as we waited for spring thaw, stuck in Slate Springs. If anything, we'd remain on the east side of the pass with her. With her.

What kind of marriage did she have before? Why was she so amazed we had been concerned? I wanted to know the answer, but not on the street. While I was big enough to keep warm in just my shirt, and the temperatures in the city were much warmer than at home, I did not think our bride could tolerate the chill for long until she became accustomed. Even then, she was a tiny thing and we needed to be cautious. If my toes were turning cold, then certainly hers were as well in her thinner shoes. Some new clothes more suited for the winter weather were our first purchases. But as I glanced down at her as we continued on, watching the gentle sway of her hips, seeing the long line of her elegant neck, I was just as eager to see her out of clothes entirely.

Celia

"This is impressive."

There weren't any other words for the suite Luke had at the hotel. I'd only come through the door, but the space was opulent. Thick rugs covered hard wood, dark red velvet curtains hung at the tall windows and also covered the chairs and couches that faced a crackling fire. I could see into two additional rooms, their doors across from each other. Large beds were centered in each, one even had a canopy. This wasn't a simple hotel room to waylay until our departure in the morning. This showed wealth. It appeared my husband had money. Lots of it.

I should be reassured that I would not be married to a pauper, but I knew that money did not offer happiness. Certainly a full belly and warm clothes, but I'd known both of those with John and I'd been so very unhappy. I would hold judgement on Luke, for now.

I watched as he removed his hat and placed it on a table by the door. He wore the usual men's uniform of dark suit, white shirt and black tie, but it seemed to fit him better than most and only accented his broad shoulders and thick chest. He turned and took his coat from my shoulders and caught me studying him. The heavy outer garment had kept me well protected from the cold and allowed his enticing scent to envelop me. Something dark and manly. Not a heavy tonic like John would have used, but a natural scent, clean and sharp. I breathed in the last remnants of it as I followed him to the couch before the fire.

I took the moment that was offered for one more surreptitious look. He was tall, so very big. I only came up to his shoulder and it should have felt imposing to have to tilt my chin back to meet his gaze, but that was not the case. Every time he spoke with me at the station and out on the street, he'd been close, perhaps a little closer than was appropriate for a man, but he was my husband. It hadn't felt awkward. Instead, I felt... protected.

Butterflies fluttered in my belly as I looked at him. His fair hair was short and neatly trimmed. His eyes, so fair and yet intense, were beneath a strong brow. His nose seemed to have a slight crook to it, as if it had been broken at one time. While it appeared he had shaved earlier in the day, whiskers dusted his square jaw and I wondered if it would feel raspy against my palm.

The entire journey from Texas I'd wondered and fretted as to the man to whom I'd been matched. Would he be just like John—a well-respected man with absolutely no conscience or values? I hadn't had to share much of my past with Mrs. Carstairs at the establishment that matched men to mail order brides. My past had preceded me certainly, but women who came to her had varied reasons for wanting to be sent to marry a stranger. I was sure she'd heard it all, even a story like mine. The underlying reason though was most likely the same. Desperation.

I had been desperate to escape Texas the only way a woman with no money or job could. That did not mean I hadn't been wary and doubting my choice for the thousand miles it took to arrive in Denver. The relief of finding Luke visually appealing was a start; however, John had been an attractive man, educated too, but a philanderer, so that did not allay all of my concerns. Only time would tell if Luke was the same.

I was wary about my attraction to him. It was instant. The moment I saw him on the station platform holding the Bible, I'd been interested. Intrigued. Immediately overwhelmed. Newfound desire had coursed through me, heating me at just the sight of him. I'd shivered when I stood before the two men. It hadn't been from cold, but the heavy feel of their attentions on me. Yes, both of them. It wasn't just Luke that had made me feel... curious, but his brother, Walker, too.

He'd been just as attentive as Luke, just as solicitous. His hair and eyes were dark, but it was obvious that they were brothers. Even in physique they were different; Walker was a touch taller and leaner. While Luke had offered a soft smile that softened the look in his eyes, Walker appeared to be more of a brooder. Intense, but no less kind.

But it was Luke who approached me now; Walker had not come to the suite with us. My heart leapt into my throat with the realization that this handsome man was my husband. Mine, and he would soon touch me, hopefully in a way I'd wanted for so long.

Without saying a word, he lifted his hands to my head, removed my hat. I breathed in his clean scent and tried to calm my racing heart. Blunt fingers ran over my hair, then tugged the pins from my prim bun.

"I've been wanting to see your hair down, to feel it," he murmured, his eyes on his ministrations.

I held myself still and let him touch me. Once all the pins were removed, my hair uncoiled and spilled long down my back. It was unruly, with a wayward curl to it. Luke grunted out what I had to hope was satisfaction as he ran his fingers through the strands. My eyes fell closed at the decadent feel of it.

"Like spun gold," he murmured. When he gently placed his hands on my shoulders, I looked up at him and watched as his eyes lowered to my mouth. "I'm going to kiss you."

"Yes," I breathed, my heart beginning to gallop like a runaway horse. I wanted that so very much.

His lips were gentle and soft. Only for a moment. Then the kiss turned carnal and deep, his tongue slipping into my mouth as I gasped. The kiss was startling, for it was like instant heat. Desire pulsed through my veins and settled between my thighs. My hands took hold of his shirt and gripped tightly as his own hands cupped my face. His palms were callused, but warm.

I had no idea how long we stood there before the fire, but Luke eventually lifted his head and I whimpered. His eyes were a dark green, narrowed and clouded with need.

I couldn't catch my breath.

"This suite has a washroom. A tub with hot water." His eyes stayed fixed on my swollen lips. "Bathe. Relax, for when you come out, I will have you well occupied."

"You... you don't have to wait," I said. My voice was unfamiliar, breathy and eager as I admitted my needs.

The corner of his mouth tipped up as his knuckles raked over my cheek. "So brave," he said with a groan. "I am not denying you. Quite the contrary. I only have so much control, sweetheart." He tilted his chin in the direction of the washroom. "I wish for you to scrub the journey from your skin, to take a minute to yourself before I possess you."

Possess. Oh God. Not take, or claim or even fuck. Possess was… more. So much more.

Offering a wobbly nod, I turned to the bathing room.

"Celia," he called.

I looked at him over my shoulder.

"When you are done, don't dress." His eyes slid down my body and I felt my nipples tighten. "I want to see you. All of you."

My cheeks heated then. He wanted to look at me, to see me bare and exposed. I should have been fearful, but it only made me… eager. If it had been anyone else who'd made such a blatant statement, I would have been mortified and appalled and fearful. But with Luke, I felt… God, aroused and eager to please.

The man was virile and dominant and yet he waited for me to accept his expectation. If I didn't, I knew somehow that he'd be gentle instead. But this was what he wanted, what he needed and would not hide that. It only made me more eager for him.

Licking my lips, I nodded and went into the other room. Leaning against the door, I caught my breath. That had just been a kiss and I was so aroused. Could I survive more?

There was no question that he wanted me, that he

would take me. Did he know that when he stopped, when he offered me a chance to bathe, it only made me more eager for him? I'd think of nothing but the kiss, of him seeing me naked for the first time. For other things. The wait was arousing.

Going to the copper tub, I adjusted the knobs until hot water poured in and I watched as the steaming water slowly filled the tub. Somehow, he had restraint, but only so much of it.

I had no idea how much time had passed once I sank into the steaming water, but he knocked once, then called my name.

"Yes?" I answered, my hands gripping the edge of the tub.

"May I come in?"

If I said no, I knew he would stay on his side of the door. I didn't even know him, yet I was confident in this, confident that he would not push me. But did I want him to stay out? I licked my lips as I knew the answer. I wanted him to come in. I wanted more kisses. I wanted... more.

"Yes," I said, my voice quiet. I was about to repeat it louder, but he heard me.

The door opened and Luke entered. His looked me in the eyes as he said, "I could not wait any longer."

I liked that he admitted to his desire, that he plainly shared the truth. It was obvious in every line of his body. His jaw was tense, his hands clenched in fists and I couldn't miss the very prominent bulge in his pants.

It was my turn now. He was waiting to see what I would do next. While I'd made the decision weeks ago to become a mail order bride, chose to board the train, this was the moment. This was the decision that made me his.

Luke wanted me. I wanted him. The connection had been instant, the attraction real. He didn't just want to take me as John had. He wanted me.

4

elia

Pushing off the sides of the tub, I stood then, letting the bath water sluice down my naked body. Let Luke look his fill. My body wasn't perfect. My breasts were on the small side, my hips wide, but the way his eyes narrowed, the way he ran a finger over his mouth made me feel beautiful.

He didn't say anything, only took a bathing towel from the chair in the corner and held it out for me. Carefully, I stepped from the tub and into his arms. He wrapped the towel about me, but instead of letting go, he lifted me into his arms and carried me into the other room, lowering me so we knelt before the fire.

"I don't want you to catch a chill," he said, now using the towel to dry me.

Slowly, he worked the towel over me, my arms, my back, then my chest as his eyes followed his motions. The soft material brushed over my breasts and I held my breath.

A groan slipped from Luke just before he lowered his head and took a nipple into his mouth. He suckled at it and I tangled my fingers in his silky hair, holding him in place. I cried out his name in a mixture of surprise and pleasure. I had no idea my nipples were so sensitive!

At my cry, Luke's restraint fell away completely. His hands moved to my body, stroked over it, pushed me back so I laid down on the soft carpet as he loomed over me. The warmth of the fire was almost too much, for his body radiated so much heat of its own. I was not cold. I knew then that whatever the weather raged outside, I would be warm in his arms.

I was breathing hard as he looked down at me, raked his gaze over my body. "I can't hold back, Celia. I wanted to be gentle our first time, but... I can't."

I shook my head. "No. Don't hold back. Please." I didn't mind begging, for I was desperate for him. His restraint had only made me more eager for him. It was as if it only built my need for him to an even greater level than if he'd taken me when we'd kissed earlier.

Now, now I ached for him. To prove to him I was not afraid, I bent my right leg and let it fall open in invitation. It was a wanton move, but Luke seemed to want me this way, to offer myself to him. My blatant interest didn't disgust him. Based on the way his jaw clenched as he looked down my body, then tugged at his pants, it only made him lose a little bit more of his control.

Opening the placket, he tugged his cock free. My eyes widened as he gripped the base and stroked himself.

"Oh God," I said. He was big. Long and thick and a pearly drop of fluid seeped from the tip. My inner walls clenched down at the idea of being stretched open for him.

He looked up at me and I saw the last vestiges of his restraint.

It would only take one word to rip it to shreds. I knew the word, whimpered it. "Please."

I wanted to be filled, taken, claimed. Possessed.

Lowering down onto a forearm, he aligned himself with my eager entrance and slowly sank into me. Unaccustomed to such girth, I shifted my hips to accommodate him. I breathed as I adjusted, grabbed hold of the back of his shirt as if I needed to hold on to something. Luke was almost too big, having to grab my hip and shift me so that his cock could slide in even deeper, then deeper still.

I loved that he was still dressed, only the important parts uncovered for him to claim me, while I was completely bare and exposed to him.

Deep inside, he held himself still as I clenched about him, only moving when I shifted my hips up.

His hand stroked my hair as he began to fuck me. Slowly, yet with vigorous intent.

"Yes!" I cried, arching my back.

It wasn't rutting as John had done. It wasn't lovemaking, for I didn't know him enough for that deep of a connection. But it was good. Oh so good and dark and carnal and rough and—

"I bet her pussy's going to milk the cum from your balls."

Walker.

My eyes flew open as I looked up at Luke's brother. I hadn't heard him come into the room. My body stiffened in surprise and I gripped Luke's back. He didn't stop moving, didn't stop fucking me. He turned his head to look up at him, but only grinned. He wasn't bothered—or surprised—that his brother had walked in on us.

Luke took my bottom in his palm and angled me so that he slid over a different spot deep inside me. My eyes slipped closed and I cried out at the delicious feel. Nothing was stopping the pleasure, not even Walker watching.

"She's perfect, brother," Luke said, breathing hard as Walker lowered himself onto a chair, let his legs sprawl out before him and watched. He was watching me being fucked! "Don't be scared, sweetheart. Let Walker see how beautiful you are."

"You are beautiful, Celia," Walker confirmed, his voice deep and rough. "So perfect beneath my brother. I can hear how wet you are for him. You're going to come, aren't you?"

I should have offended by Walker's appearance, by Luke's casual attitude, should have pushed at him so I could run away in shame. I should have at least wanted to cover myself. But I didn't.

"My cock is rock hard looking at you," Walker crooned, as if he knew his words made me hotter. "Seeing the pleasure on your face, watching your nipples tighten. I bet your pussy's so sweet and tight."

"I'm going to... God, it's too much," I said.

"Shh," Luke crooned. "I've got you. Let go, sweetheart. Come all over my cock."

My head thrashed from side to side as I tried to get to a place, somewhere that I couldn't reach. The pleasure was too much, so intense that I was afraid that it would overwhelm me.

"Walker wants to see you when you come."

Those words were what pushed me over. I tensed, then every muscle in my body went lax beneath Luke's weight, my bones seemed to have dissolved. I cried out my pleasure as my hands fell to my sides. "Luke!" I cried again, overcome.

Luke plunged deep, once, then twice, then stilled deep inside. He groaned as I felt his seed fill me.

He lowered his head to my neck and our wild breaths mingled before he pushed off and moved to lie beside me.

I smiled to myself, reveling in the bliss that Luke had

wrung from my body. John had never done that to me. I'd never felt that way when he'd touched me. No other man had—

My eyes opened. "Oh God!" I cried, tilting my head to look up at Walker. Grabbing the bathing towel that lay on the floor beneath me, I tugged at it to try to cover myself without much success.

Walker stared down at me, completely at ease, his hat in his hands. He wore a suit and tie similar to his brother's. Formal while I was naked, sweaty and dripping with his brother's seed.

"I've asked for food to be delivered. Shouldn't take too long."

He spoke as if he hadn't witnessed something so private, so carnal. I was confused by my reactions, or lack of. The fire at my side was too much. I felt overheated and Luke was doing nothing to shelter me or cover me from his brother's eyes. He didn't seem to be cruel about it, more that he was willing to share me with him, that he wanted to show me off.

I scrambled to my feet, ran to the nearest bedroom and shut the door behind me, leaned against the hard surface. The wood was cool against my palms, my bare back, as I tried to catch my breath. I was naked and I felt Luke's seed slip down my thighs.

I'd fucked my husband while his brother watched!

I put my hands over my face and wondered what I'd turned into. I'd wanted to be more daring, to feel the pleasure that could be had in a marriage, but this was nothing I'd ever imagined. I was so wicked and wanton. It wasn't because I was surprised that he'd watched, but I was surprised that I'd liked it.

"Oh God," I whispered, shaking my head.

I stared at the bed and realized this was not a good place to hide. I wasn't going to just bed Luke tonight. The way Walker had been looking at me, the way Luke had allowed it, he was just as interested. The connection between us was just as strong as with Luke and me.

"Celia." Luke's voice was deep, yet calm. "Open the door."

I took a few deep breaths and realized I had to face them. I'd let John have his way, turned my head at the signs that he had strayed from our marital bed, that when we knew no children would come from our union, he'd never considered me anything more than a free source of labor for his practice. It had been my fault.

And now, I'd gotten myself into this situation with Luke and Walker. I'd chosen to be a mail order bride. Of course, I was going to be wedded and bedded. I'd known that all along. I wasn't twenty anymore. I wasn't young or naive, but never in my wildest and most tawdry thoughts did I imagine Luke sharing me with his brother.

I couldn't stay in this room forever. I knew the limit of Luke's patience and he would eventually open the door on his own. I could not keep him out. But he was waiting for me to come out voluntarily. I had to face them. I'd been silent for one marriage, and look what that had done to my life. I wouldn't be silent in this one.

Grabbing the blanket off the foot of the big bed, I wrapped it about my shoulders, about to face two very ardent men. After one more deep breath, I turned and opened the door. Both men loomed and were quite daunting. Both of their gazes raked over my blanket-covered body. For one heartbeat, I feared they would push their way into the bedroom and have their way with me, but they didn't. I saw nothing but concern on their faces.

Luke's cock was tucked back in his pants and he showed no outward signs of just having fucked besides his hair being unruly. I remembered the silky feel of those strands.

I breathed through my mouth as I tried to calm my racing heart.

Luke began to undo the buttons of his shirt, tugged the tails from his pants and stripped it off. "Here." He held it out for me to take. "You will be more comfortable in my shirt than the blanket."

I took the garment, still warm from his body, then closed the door behind me, slipped it on in privacy and buttoned it up. It was big on me, so big that it hung down almost to my knees.

Opening the door once more, Luke smiled. "Looks better on you than me. Please, Celia. Sit." Luke's voice was even more gentle than before. I took in his bare chest and I swallowed. A smattering of light hair was on his broad chest. It tapered to a V toward his navel and then even lower. Muscles rippled and I wanted to feel every defined inch of him. Resisting the urge—he'd just fucked me minutes ago—I clenched my hands into fists.

They stepped back so I could pass and I moved to the couch across from the fire and sat down, careful to tug the shirt down over my thighs. The men sat down on either side of me, their legs pressed into mine. I was surrounded.

"Mrs. Carstairs shared little about you in her telegram," Luke began. "That you are a widow."

I frowned at him, confused. "After what just happened, you want to know that?"

Luke looked a little chagrined. "Perhaps we should have done this first."

I looked down at my lap as I felt my cheeks heat, wondering what else she'd shared. Hopefully the heat from the fire hid that from them. "Yes, perhaps," I replied, not wishing to offer up too many details. I didn't wish for him to think any less of me. "And yes, I'm a widow."

"I'm sorry for your loss," Walker said. I tilted my head and offered him a small smile. "No children, then."

It wasn't a question, for the answer was obvious since no toddlers alighted the train with me. Still, I shook my head at another one of my wifely inadequacies.

"Were you happy, Celia?" Luke asked. His voice was gentle, but I still felt surrounded, pressured, so I stood, moved to stand and look down at the crackling fire. With the sleeves dangling over my hands, I kept myself busy by rolling them up to my wrists.

"Was it a love match, you mean?" I didn't turn to look

at the men for an answer, and neither responded, obviously allowing me to take my time. "I thought so, at first. But I was quite young and didn't know what love was. I knew he was independent and expected me to be as well."

"We are not overbearing either."

Overbearing? No, Luke hadn't been overbearing. Bold, yes.

I heard the word "we" in his sentence but did not give it much credence. I straightened my spine and lifted my chin. "I won't be a simpering wife, I assure you."

"No, I don't think you will," Luke replied. "We are possessive men, though, Celia, and will ensure to your safety and wellbeing. We will allow you independence, but you will find us very protective of what belongs to us."

I spun about then, the heat from the fire at my back. "What?"

"We are very protective," Walker repeated.

"We?" I looked between the two. Both had earnest expressions. Open. They were relaxed, their gazes fixed on me. "Um... I don't understand."

"Besides being a mine owner, I am also the mayor of Slate Springs," Luke shared. "As I said, the town is isolated in the winter and the population is predominantly male. A new law has been passed."

A hint of apprehension appeared in Luke's gaze, then was gone. I had to wonder if I imagined it.

"The law allows for two men to marry the same woman."

My mouth fell open as I glanced between the two brothers. "You mean... I am—"

"The reason why I watched you and Luke fuck—why he allowed me to do so—is because you are married to both of us," Walker finished for me.

5

elia

"I should have told you this before we... well, before I took you, but I couldn't resist and I had no patience to wait for Walker."

The corner of Luke's mouth turned up and I saw the look of satisfaction on his face. I'd put that there.

"Neither could you," he added.

I looked down at my bare feet.

"No, neither could I," I admitted. I'd wanted him something fierce. I still did.

"There was no way to ease you into the arrangement, to take our time and tell you, so we felt it best if—"

A knock at the door interrupted him.

Luke swore under his breath and Walker went to open it.

A uniformed porter rolled in a cloth-covered tray with dishes covered with silver domes. I spun on my heel and faced away from the man, Luke coming to stand before me, to block me from view. My cheeks flushed, wondering what the porter thought of me. Could he know that I was married to both Luke and Walker? Could he tell I'd just fucked Luke? God, of course he could. I was wearing Luke's shirt!

I knew scandal, was too familiar with it, and didn't wish to have another. But the man took the tip Walker offered and closed the door behind him without a word.

Luke put his hand on my shoulder and turned me toward the table. My nipples pebbled against the soft fabric of his shirt and seed still slid from me.

"While I will share you with Walker, we will not allow another to look upon you as we do," Luke said.

"Perhaps it is better to eat as we talk," Walker suggested, lifting a cover from a dish. A large, very pink steak was revealed, then glazed carrots, mashed potatoes and more as the plates were uncovered.

"You have just revealed that I am married to both of you and you expect me to sit and eat?" They seemed too calm about this, or perhaps they'd just had more time to reconcile to the idea.

Using a serving spoon, Walker put a variety of items onto the plate with the steak and carried it to the dining table that sat before a large bay window. I had to imagine the view if it were daytime.

"Please," he said, waving his hand to the plate. "You said you were hungry after your journey."

I was hungry and the topic of conversation wasn't going to change regardless of whether I ate or not. Walker held out the chair for me before turning to the food cart for himself. Luke pulled out the chair beside me, spun it about and sat down with his legs straddling the seat. His bare forearms rested on the chair back and he watched me as I cut a slice of meat, then put it in my mouth.

"Slate Springs has a population of about three thousand," he began. "Only three hundred or so are women. All of them are either married, much older than the bachelors or too young to wed. A young maiden who arrives in town is snatched up quickly, usually with at least two fights beforehand. With the town being isolated for five months a year, the men become… aggressive and somewhat volatile by the end of winter."

He meant they hadn't been able to fuck a woman for that stretch, but I didn't clarify.

"Once the pass opens, most of the men are eager to leave town, never to return. As a business owner, it is a concern since my miners have walked away from their jobs, but there is a never-ending line of men ready to work. Replacements are easy to come by."

"But the town does not grow, nor have a large number of families," Walker added. He'd sat on the other side of him and made quick work of his carrots. He speared another. "They are quite good. Try one."

He coaxed me into eating a buttery sweet carrot and I nodded in agreement. The food on the journey had been passable at best. This was the first meal I'd had in weeks where I didn't have to eat quickly when the train stopped for more water and coal, or eat alone.

"The solution was to allow two men to marry the same woman," Walker added, when he was satisfied I'd eaten the vegetable.

"I can't imagine everyone would be keen on this idea. Surely the clergy would find it amoral," I added, cutting another piece of steak. My stomach had settled after the men's initial surprise and I realized I was ravenous. I was glad for the food, and something to do as we spoke. Was this why Walker had suggested it?

"There are some who are against the law, but they are either wed already or are, as you say, in the clergy. The Bible was separated from the challenge the town council faced."

"And yet you used it to identify yourself to me on the platform," I countered.

Walker grinned, pointed his fork at me. "Touché."

"Most men in Slate Springs want a bride, but they are few and far between." Luke snared a roll from Walker's plate, ripped it in half and popped a piece into his mouth.

"Thus, your need for a mail order bride," I added. "I assume the other men will need to leave town to find a bride?"

A Wanton Woman

"Yes." Luke shifted in his seat. "As mayor, everyone in Slate Springs is looking to me to set an example, to ensure the law works before others are willing to commit."

"So I am wanted solely as an experiment?" I knew Luke had not specifically chosen me, personally, from Mrs. Carstairs' business. He'd wanted a woman who would wed him sight unseen. I shouldn't have felt hurt by the truth because I'd known it all along, but still, I was.

Luke didn't answer the question. Instead, he asked one of his own. "And what of you? You must have a reason for choosing to become a mail order bride."

I was very thankful then for the food on my plate. I took a big bite of carrot and took my time to chew, stalling.

I glanced at the men, who recognized my action for what it was, but remained quiet and patient. Waiting.

"My husband died and left me without money. While I have skills as a nurse, my chances for a job were limited in Tyler." Especially with my history and the gossip that followed. "I felt it was best to move somewhere else."

That was vague and did not cast any light to the real reasons for my departure. Pleased with myself, I took a sip of water.

"We are businessmen, Celia. We can bullshit better than most," Walker said, not softening his words. "Luke's the mayor and this kind of vague talk is his strength."

"That's right, sweetheart," Luke added. "You've probably been raised not to share your burdens, being diplomatic and aloof. I appreciate a woman who can keep a secret, but we're your husbands. There will be no secrets between us."

Husbands. Instead of being standoffish, they wanted me to bare all.

The mashed potatoes on my tongue tasted like sawdust and I worked hard to swallow them down.

"Let me ask you more specific questions and that are easier to answer," Walker said, placing his fork and knife on his plate. "How long were you married?"

"Five years."

"From your clothing, it does not appear as if you were destitute in your marriage. Is that correct?"

"Yes," I answered, then took a moment to study him. "You sound like a lawyer."

Walker smiled then, brilliantly, showing off straight white teeth and a face so handsome my breath caught. "That's right. You have me figured out, doll. Now let's do the same with you."

"What was your husband's profession?" Luke asked.

"He was a doctor."

"Impressive. And you were his nurse?"

I nodded.

"How did he die?"

I bit my lip, recognizing Walker had started off with easy questions and they were quickly becoming more difficult to answer. Using my napkin, I wiped my mouth.

"He was shot."

Both men's eyes widened.

"I'm sorry to hear that," Walker murmured. "You must miss him keenly."

I pushed back my chair at the ridiculous notion, then stood. "What about you, Walker?" I asked, steering the conversation away from me. "Why did you agree to this unusual marriage?" I pointed to the two of them as they stood as well. They certainly had good manners.

"To be honest, I want a woman in my bed every night."

His bluntness caught me by surprise. "So no interest in a love match then?"

He tossed his napkin on the table, moved to pace the room. "I am a widower."

I could hear the darkness in his voice, see the tenseness in his shoulders.

"Marrying again was not something I ever considered. But the new law forced Luke's hand into marriage." He shrugged, then turned to look at me. "It offered me the opportunity I had never considered before."

"Oh?"

"A woman deserves love in a marriage. Fair warning, you won't get that from me. Not because I don't think you are deserving, but because I just don't have it to give. But you'll get that from Luke. I'll give you everything else: my protection, my money, my attention. My body."

The idea of having continuous and permanent access to Walker's body was definitely enticing, but it wasn't enough. Wiping my hand over my face, I laughed, although without any amusement. "None of us want this. Luke, you're marrying me out of duty—"

"I didn't just fuck you out of duty," Luke said, cutting off my words. "As for want, you wanted me as much as I wanted you."

I could not argue, for it was true.

"Walker, you're... marrying me for a lifetime of fucking."

He ran a hand over the back of his neck. "Based on what I watched, it does not appear it will be a hardship for either of us."

"All of us," Luke clarified. "What about you, Celia? You deflected our questions. It's time to bare all, sweetheart."

He moving to lean against the back of the couch, arms crossed.

"I am the only one who has bared everything," I countered, meaning I'd been naked while he'd remained fully dressed. They were not swayed by that diversion tactic and I sighed. "You want to know how my husband died?"

Luke offered a simple "yes," then waited.

"My husband was shot in our marriage bed as he was fucking his mistress. The woman's husband discovered their illicit activities and found them together. Killed them both."

"Fuck," Walker murmured, shaking his head.

"He left you without money?"

I glanced at both men, then away. They seemed more angry than upset.

"The house and any money in the bank went to his nephew."

"Couldn't you have worked as a nurse for another doctor?"

Putting my hands on my hips, I stared at Luke, narrowed my eyes. "You're thinking like a man."

"What doctor would hire a woman whose husband had been murdered, you mean," Luke replied.

Walker shook his head. "No, it was worse than that, wasn't it, doll? They blamed you. The husband, the town, everyone."

Tears filled my eyes, but I blinked them away, refused to meet either of their gazes. I was used to John being distracted, never offering me his full attention. But with Luke and Walker, theirs didn't waver and I was uncomfortable beneath their scrutiny.

"Ah, Celia," Luke whispered.

I dropped my hands to my sides. "I should have been a better wife. Kept him happy. Gave him children. Satisfied so he wouldn't stray."

"There was something wrong with your husband, sweetheart, not you. Look at you." Luke lifted his hand and his eyes grazed over my body. "You're beautiful. You came alive in my arms, on my cock. Any man in his right mind would want you. Hell, I couldn't even wait ten minutes."

"I want you, too," Walker added, putting a hand to the front of his pants and rubbing his cock.

I blushed at their words, thinking of how bold I'd been, how while I'd been bothered at first that Walker had walked in on Luke and me, I'd liked it.

"Without means, without a job and your name in disgrace, you decided to become a mail order bride," Walker finished, breaking me from my carnal thoughts.

What he said was all true. Every bit of it. He wasn't being cruel by saying it aloud, only honest.

But from my recounting, I'd left out Carl Norman, the brother of the man who'd killed John and his mistress. As I'd witnessed Neil Norman's crime, my testimony had sealed his fate and he'd been hung within the week. Carl had first accosted me two days after the hanging and had dogged me about town ever since, blaming me for his brother's death, threatening to kill me.

I'd been the one who'd let my husband stray. If I'd been a better wife, more attentive sexually and provided him with children, he would have been content with me. But no. He'd been forced to find comfort elsewhere. As he'd dragged me into an alley and pinned me there with a hand about my neck, I wasn't going to tell him that perhaps the problem had lain with his brother, who obviously hadn't been able to satisfy his wife.

While I'd fled Tyler because I had no reputation left, I also feared for my life. I'd been watching over my shoulder for Carl ever since. While the finger-shaped bruises about my neck had faded, the worry had not. I'd known he was watching, waiting for the moment to do me harm. In his anger, I thought he would follow me from Tyler, perhaps do something like toss me off the moving train. It was an easy and very tidy way to kill someone, a body left to rot out on the open prairie of west Texas or Oklahoma where no one would ever find it. In my case, no one would miss me or question my disappearance. No one cared.

When I stepped onto the train platform in Denver, I'd been relieved. But it didn't allay my fears entirely, as he could follow on a later train. I would always be looking over my shoulder as I knew he would not be deterred.

The news that Luke and Walker's town would be snowed in for a few months had been almost joyful. That meant Carl couldn't get to me. Perhaps in that time he'd either calm his anger or give up.

"None of us wanted this marriage," I said, admitting the truth.

Luke and Walker remained silent.

"You can annul, you know," I continued. "I'll stay here in Denver and find a job. I'm sure my nursing skills are needed."

6

elia

Luke pushed off the back of the couch and stood abruptly.

"No." Both men spoke at the same time, their voices loud, commanding.

I took a step backward, surprised by the instant vehemence.

"No?" I asked, licking my lips.

"While we may have not wanted to marry, we want you," Luke said, glancing at his brother, who nodded. "Didn't I just prove that in front of the fire? You're wearing my shirt." He pointed at my skimpy attire. "My seed is dripping down your thighs. Hell, you came with Walker watching. I'd say you want us, too."

I blushed furiously.

"Unlike your first husband, we are honorable. We don't stray. We aren't anything like him, doll," Walker added.

I laughed then, as there was no comparison between the thin, pale man I'd married five years ago and these two strapping cowboys. "No, no, you're nothing alike. But I was only married to one man, not two."

"You have reservations," Luke said.

"I have questions," I countered. "Such as, how does it work?"

"Being married to two men?" Walker asked. "This is a first for us, as well. First for the town, too. I think we can make this marriage work any way we wish."

I bit my lip. "Yes, but... I meant in the, um... bedroom, specifically."

Luke's eyes widened, then he smiled. "You enjoyed fucking me, sweetheart?"

I nodded, because I couldn't lie. They were both witness to my first pleasure.

"Being married to both of us gets you two men to give you pleasure."

He said it so simply, so easily, confident that they could both satisfy me.

I flushed hotly and turned away, looked blindly down at the food on the table.

"What do you want, Celia?" Luke asked. "What do you want from a marriage? You've been married and know what it's like, what you were missing. What is it you'd hoped for? We'll give it to you."

I felt frayed, my emotions revealed. The scars of my first marriage ached and Walker and Luke seemed to know how to expose every single one. I picked up a fork, studied the detail work in the silver. "How can you say that? How can you know what I want?"

"Is it money? You never have to worry about going hungry, I promise you," Luke said.

"Is it protection?" Walker asked. "No harm will come to you when you are with us."

I thought of how Luke had hidden me from the porter's view.

An ache filled my chest. That was what I wanted so very badly, to know that they would take care of me, that the bad things in the world, like Carl Norman, would never affect me. But they couldn't protect me from my past. No one could.

"Tell us, sweetheart," Luke prodded.

Was it as simple as just telling them my wants and they would give them to me? It was never that simple. I'd wanted a marriage with at least mutual respect, but John didn't respect me. I'd known him for some time before we wed, but these men. I knew nothing about them. And yet they could promise to fulfill my every desire?

A knot of frustration and anger formed in my chest. My hands clenched into fists. If they wanted to know what I wanted, then I'd tell them. What did it matter at this point? When they announced Walker was also my husband, it seemed civilized rules didn't matter. And so I opened my mouth and told them.

I spun about, lifted my chin and said, "I want a man who won't ignore me. Who will smile at me and offer reasonable conversation. I want a man who is respectful and courteous. I want more than a man to give me food and shelter. I want a husband."

"You get two, then, doll, who will do all that," Walker said when I took a breath.

I held up my hand. "I'm not done. I want someone who is all mine. To share secrets and laugh."

Once I began, it was easy to just let it all out, to share what I wanted. That's why I didn't stop.

"I also want to be fucked, well and good. I don't want it at night, in the dark. I don't want a quick rut, then nothing. I want fulfillment, wild abandon." I thought of John's mistress, how she'd loved what he'd been doing to her before they were discovered. "I want to be tied up. Taken. Do things I never even imagined."

I was breathing hard, my skin hot and prickly. There, I'd said it. I'd said exactly what I wanted, everything I never said to John.

Both men's gazes darkened and turned intense.

"I'm proud of you for sharing that. It must have been hard for you to admit the last," Walker said, his words of praise acting like a balm. "You had a taste of what it will be like with Luke. While it was a quick rut, it was wild and full of abandon."

I felt the soreness of our actions between my thighs, unaccustomed to a man of his size and his... vigor.

"Yes. That's true." I shook my head slowly. "But I won't be married to a man... to men, who stray. I won't be cast aside again. If I'm not enough, turn me away now."

"Turn you away?" Luke asked. "I'll turn you over my knee if you even think about walking out that door."

My eyes widened and I felt my cheeks heat at the idea of being placed in such a position. I remembered John's mistress and how she'd liked it when he'd spanked her bare bottom. The sound of it, that skin against skin crack and then a fiery burst of stinging pain. I wanted that. I wanted to know what it was like. I wanted to know it all.

"I can see that excites you. Doesn't it, sweetheart?" Luke asked.

I bit my lip, wondering if I should admit the truth. The truth, though, was well and truly out, so what was the point of denying it now? And so I nodded.

Luke stepped toward me, but I held still, not letting him know I was a little wary. I wasn't afraid of them, but I'd never been completely honest with John, never shared the darkest of secrets with him. The truth was powerful and so I wondered what they would say... or do, next.

"We'll never want another," he murmured.

His tone was even, his voice earnest.

I looked up at him, saw the serious expression. "How can you say that? I... I didn't please John. I won't have you fuck me then find me lacking. I'd rather you decide you don't want me now, before... before I have feelings."

"Lacking?" Luke asked. "Walker, when you were watching me fuck our bride, did it look like I found Celia lacking?"

"Hell, no. Woman," Walker growled. "We'll say it one last time. You'll stay and we won't stray."

The vehemence of his tone had me believing him, but the doubt still lingered. "I—"

"You've given this worry to us. Let it go," Luke added. The back of his knuckles stroked down my cheek and I shivered. "You want us to take control, to give you what you need."

Did I? Did I want them to take my worries away? Was that why I told them those secrets? Was it so that they could know the truth and want me anyway, to do exactly what I wanted?

My gaze met his, then skittered over his shoulder to look at the decorative wallpaper. "How can you do that, give me what I need, I mean, when... when I don't even know what I need?"

Walker moved closer. I had one man in front of me, the other at my side, Walker's big hand gentle on my shoulder. "We'll discover it together. Enough for tonight. You're exhausted and we've given you quite a surprise. While I desperately want to feel the heat of your pussy around my cock, I'm sure you're a little tender. Hmm?"

Would I ever stop blushing? "Yes," I admitted.

"Tomorrow is soon enough," he said, pulling me into his arms. He felt different than Luke, his scent was different.

7

elia

I was so warm, overly so and I tried to push the heavy blanket off of me. When I put my hands over me to move it away, it wasn't a blanket, but an arm. My breath caught and my heart skipped before I remembered. Luke and Walker. I was in bed with one of them.

Glancing down, I saw an arm, sprinkled with dark hair, about my waist. Based on the hair color on the arm, it was Walker. The hand was so big, it reached from my hipbone to have the thumb brush the underside of my breast. My bare breast. I'd worn Luke's shirt to bed, but it had ridden up well past my waist and Walker's hand was beneath it.

It all came back to me then. Arriving in Denver, the

luxurious hotel room, the men's pressure into having me admit hard truths, the fucking. God, the fucking.

The blanket had fallen about my waist and I was pressed against a solid wall of man, his front against my back like two spoons in a drawer. I felt every hard inch of him. The hair on his chest tickled my back, his strong thighs tucked behind mine. That meant the hardness pressing against my bottom was his—

"Don't be frightened, doll."

Walker's voice was rough and deep from sleep.

I should have been frightened. I was in a stranger's bed, in his arms, practically naked. I'd done such wicked and carnal things with his brother.

A whimper escaped just before he shifted so that I was on my back and he was looming over me, settled up onto one forearm. He began to undo the buttons down the front of the shirt, slowly exposing me, inch by inch.

I looked up at Walker. His dark hair, which last night had been neatly combed, fell over his forehead, tousled from sleep. His shoulders were so broad he blocked out the pale light coming in from the window. His eyes were on the skin that he was exposing.

"Sleep well?" he asked, as he parted the fabric so it fell off to the sides. Except for my arms, I was bare to him.

I heated at his honest and blatant perusal. Had I slept well? Yes. I hadn't slept that well in a long time. I barely remember being tucked beneath the covers and Walker climbing into bed and pulling me into his arms. I remembered Luke settling on the other side of me, but nothing more.

I nodded.

He smiled then and the harsh edges he bore the night before were gone. "Good. You had a long trip and if you weren't weary enough from that, Luke certainly wore you out."

I flushed then and he grinned broadly, as he brushed one finger across my collarbones.

"You turn pink when you're embarrassed. Everywhere."

I looked away from his mesmerizing eyes. "Where's Luke?"

His hand stilled. "Are you afraid of me?"

"No. I just... wondered."

Walker sighed. "He had an errand to run but will be back soon." He glanced over his shoulder to the window. "The weather is fair again today, but there are clouds over the mountains, which means it's snowing up there. While I wanted to stay at least a day, if not two, with you in this bed, we need to get home."

My mind cleared then and I remembered Carl Norman. "Oh!"

I tried to move away from Walker, but he didn't shift. Big as he was, I wouldn't be able to get up unless he let me. The idea of him keeping me in bed—of wanting me beneath him—was quite nice, for John had never even held me. Not once. But the longer we remained in Denver, the chance of Carl finding me grew. While I couldn't be sure he would follow through with his threats, I couldn't ignore them. I had to keep moving. The sooner we were in Slate Springs and the pass closed behind us, the better.

"Yes, we should hurry."

Walker moved his arm and I pushed up and slid to the side of the bed. Sitting up, I realized I had no covers, no way to shield myself except to tug the sides of Luke's shirt together, but it still gaped open. While he'd seen me the night before, naked and beneath Luke, the morning light hid nothing.

Glancing over my shoulder, I saw that Walker hadn't moved, just remained relaxed and comfortable as he watched me. While he had a gleam in his eye that indicated interest, he was not making any kind of advances. He did not seem the least bit bothered by waking up with a woman he barely knew.

"You seem quite at ease. Is this something you do often?" I bit my lip as soon as the words escaped, for they were sharply barbed and not deserved.

Walker's eyes narrowed, but he did not offer any other indication that he was bothered. He studied me quietly for some time, long enough for me to want to squirm under the intensity of it.

"Jealous, doll?"

My mouth fell open. "What? No! I shouldn't have said... I mean it was... let me up."

"I am not keeping you in bed."

"Yes, but I need more than Luke's shirt."

"I'd rather you didn't cover yourself at all, for you are quite lovely. Ah, the blush again." He smiled softly and I refused to look down at my chest where I knew it was turning as pink as my cheeks. "I was no virgin coming into this marriage, and neither were you. We have both been married before. I have vowed to be true to you and I will, but we can't make the past go away. What I did before you is of no consequence."

I sighed and studied him. He was not apologizing for any women he'd been with before, for he had no reason to do so. He was correct. What he did before my arrival was of no consequence. He was also correct in that my shrewish questioning was out of jealousy.

"I'm sorry." It was simple, but enough, for he nodded.

"To answer your question, I am at ease because I am happy. I find I am enjoying being married again very much."

"But we haven't... I mean—"

"Fucked?" he asked. "You had no problem with the word last night, doll." He tugged gently on the tail of Luke's shirt, but not hard enough to pull it from my grasp. It was enough for me to know he could easily strip me bare, and more than with words. "Say it."

"Fucked," I murmured.

"Good girl. We will fuck soon enough," he vowed. "And I enjoyed sleeping with you in my arms. Did Luke not please you?"

I pursed my lips. "You have forced my hand. How can I deny that he did? How can I deny that I didn't enjoy it?"

A Wanton Woman

His grin returned. "And yet you are afraid that I will find you... what?"

"A whore," I whispered, looking away.

His eyes narrowed. "I do not like that term, or the way you are thinking of yourself. If you speak of yourself thusly again, I will take you over my knee."

I was taken aback by his vehemence and didn't know what to say.

"Doll, enjoying what your husbands do with you in bed—or out—does not make you a whore."

I bit my lip. "But I've never liked it before now."

I was mortified by our conversation. John and I never spoke of such things. Perhaps that was one of our problems. If he'd known I'd been dissatisfied, would he have changed his ways? I thought of his strict routine and casual view on our marriage. Most likely, he wouldn't have done a thing differently. It probably would have driven him into the arms of another woman even sooner.

Walker reached out and tugged me back down beneath him, breaking me from my thoughts about John. His dark gaze searched my face once again. I couldn't help the tear that escaped. With his thumb, Walker wiped it away.

"You give us quite the compliment," he said. "Your husband couldn't please you and that's a sad thing. You came hard last night for Luke." I turned my head away but Walker tilted my cheek back so I couldn't look away. "You came because he gave you what you needed. You can't compare, doll. I promise you, Luke and I will not just fuck you beneath the covers in the dark. We're going to do things with you that will surprise you, make you question everything you used to know."

I heard a door open, close, then heavy footfalls.

"Luke's returned."

Within seconds, he filled the open bedroom doorway.

I saw that my shirt had fallen open and my breasts were exposed, the soft hairs of Walker's chest tickling my belly. Luke's gaze raked over both of us as he shrugged out of his coat and I could only imagine what he was thinking.

He tossed it on the back of a settee, sat down and tugged off his boots.

"Was your outing successful, brother?" Walker asked, not moving off of me.

"It was." Luke stood to his formidable height and reached into his coat pocket. With his back to us, I couldn't see what he'd retrieved.

"While we were sleeping, doll, Luke went and collected a few items that we couldn't get in Slate Springs." Walker moved so that he was sitting up in bed, leaning against the pillows, as casual and relaxed as ever.

The sheet rode low on his waist and I took in his torso. While I'd woken in his arms and felt his chest, this was the first time I'd actually seen it.

He was so much bigger and heavier than John, with corded muscles beneath dark skin. A smattering of hair was on his chest between flat, dark nipples. He was leaner even than Luke, but no less appealing.

Luke cleared his throat and I blushed furiously, caught ogling Walker's chest. I tugged the shirt closed. Both of them grinned at me.

"Remember last night when you asked us how our marriage would work? We said you'd be pleasured by two men."

"Yes," I replied. "I remember."

"I took you without Walker. He'll fuck you on occasion without me. Sometimes, we'll take you one after the other." Luke cocked his head to the side.

I could feel myself flush and I had to wonder if I'd ever stop being embarrassed. But it was tempered by their calm demeanors and the hint of need in their gazes. They were as affected as I. They wanted it, too. Needed it.

"Soon, we'll take you together."

"At the same time," Walker added.

I glanced at him, then Luke, trying to understand what they meant.

"I'll take your pussy," Luke told me.

"And I'll take your ass."

The shirt slipped a little from my fingers as I realized what they meant. Swallowing hard, I licked my lips. "You mean... together?"

That's what he'd said before, but I hadn't realized together meant *together*.

Luke nodded.

"But... but you're both so big. I've never—" I shook my head. "It won't work."

Walker offered a very manly grunt. "Oh, it will, doll. We just have to prepare you."

Turning my head, I looked at Walker. His expression was so open, so relaxed. How could he feel that way when talking about doing something so…wrong.

"It's shameful, all of it. This talk, how I behaved last night," I admitted, looking down at the bed. "I let you watch as he… as he fucked me."

Walker reached out and tugged me toward him, this time with enough strength that I fell into him with a small gasp of surprise.

Wrapping his arms around me, he pulled me up so I lay atop his chest. The sheet was between us, Walker beneath and me on top. He tugged at Luke's shirt and easily stripped it from me, tossed it onto the floor.

"Walker!" I cried, trying to move, but he held me in place, one hand at my lower back, the other on my neck. His hold wasn't harsh, but insistent.

"You need to listen, doll. We've said it before and we'll say it again and again until you understand. What we do together is not shameful. Giving each other pleasure is not shameful or embarrassing. Sharing your desires, telling us what makes you hot, what will make you come makes you such a good girl."

Luke came over to the side of the bed, squatted down so he could look me straight in the eye. He was so handsome, his fair hair creased with a line from his hat. His cheeks were clean shaven, as if he'd risen much earlier and shaved. His scent was different than Walker's.

Like fresh air and some wood smoke. Walker was more sharp spice. Together, their merged scent was heady and so very masculine.

Beneath my cheek, I heard the steady beat of Walker's heart, his heat seeping into me. Unlike John's calm demeanor where he'd used silence to unnerve me, I felt that these two men were patient and steady, as if allowing me time to contemplate our discussion and to understand them. To understand us.

"It's our privilege as your husbands to give you exactly what you need. Just as you will for us," Luke added.

8

elia

"But I don't think I'm going to like having you take me there," I admitted. "It will surely hurt."

Luke smiled, the lines at the corners of his eyes crinkling. "Thank you for telling us how you feel," he said. They'd said that before, as if they were refreshed by my honesty. He placed his elbow on the mattress and held a small object aloft for me to see. "It would definitely hurt if we fucked your ass now. Our cocks are big and you're not prepared."

I frowned at the oddly shaped piece of wood. It looked like a sock darner, but the tip was more pointed, and it was smaller. "Prepared?" Walker had said that word before, but had yet to answer me.

Walker's hand slid up my back again, then down; it didn't stop at the base of my spine, but moved lower to cup my bottom. His thumb slipped into the seam between and brushed over my—

I gasped.

"Your ass, doll, needs to be ready for our cocks. You're so tight here, we need to open you up."

I startled at the feel of Walker's thumb there again. He brushed it over that sensitive skin so lightly.

"Shh," he crooned. "Does this hurt?"

I shook my head against his chest. It didn't hurt, but felt pleasurable and decadent. Wicked. He shifted a leg, which moved mine apart, opening me up even further for him.

"We won't hurt you. We'll never hurt you. Only pleasure."

"But—"

Luke moved to sit on the side of the bed. He put the wooden object down and slipped a hand between my legs, below Walker's. His fingers slipped over my folds as Walker continued to touch me in that forbidden place.

My eyes slipped closed at their erotic touch.

As Walker continued to lightly circle my bottom, Luke slipped a finger into my pussy.

"I can feel my seed." Luke groaned. "I'm hard, Celia, knowing your pussy's marked by me, and soon by Walker, too."

The pleasure, the need, was instant. I was so sensitive inside that Luke's finger made me cry out. My hips shifted, which pushed Walker's thumb harder against my untried hole. It didn't hurt. Quite the opposite actually.

"Ride our fingers, doll. Rub your clit on me. Yes, like that."

It was easy to slip into need, to forget that I was naked on top of one man as his thumb was insistent on gaining entry to my virgin bottom while another finger fucked my well-used pussy. I wanted to come, to feel like I had the night before. And so I moved my hips, rubbed that bundle of nerves Walker called a clit against the sheet. All the while, the men moved their fingers about.

Walker's thumb moved away briefly to slide over my inner thigh, then returned, coated in my arousal. It made the digit slippery and when he pushed gently against that tender opening, it flowered open for him, if only just a little bit.

I cried out at the odd sensation of being stretched, but it wasn't bad. In fact, it felt really, really good. So good that I moved my hips even more, which only slid his thumb in even a tiny bit further. He didn't move it, just kept it still, stretching me, letting me adjust to the feeling of something there, even if just negligibly.

It made my hands clench the hard muscles of Walker's arms as I lifted and lowered my hips, circled them. It was so warm in the room that sweat broke out on my skin. I knew what it felt like to come now and I was close.

Walker murmured dirty little things in my ears, about how he couldn't wait to open my ass up more with the plug. Luke whispered about how much I liked their touch, how much he couldn't wait to get his cock back inside my tight heat.

Everything coalesced into bright, hot need and when Luke curled his finger in some magical way, I came. Nothing could hold it back. Nothing could hold back my scream of pleasure either as I clenched down on them inside me, as if my body didn't want them to leave, but wanted them deeper instead.

Walker's thumb slipped from me first, his other hand sliding up and down my sweaty back. Luke moved his finger in a way that wrung the last bit of pleasure from my body. Only then did he pull away. I moaned at the loss, for while I enjoyed the dexterity of his finger, it wasn't enough. It wasn't long enough or thick enough. I needed his cock.

"Luke," I moaned as he stood and began to strip, eager to join us in bed.

I watched as his body was quickly exposed. He was heavier than his brother; where Walker was lean, Luke's build was more muscular and solid. His hips were narrow and I didn't even take a moment to look at his legs, for his cock was right there. It was thick and long as I remembered it, but the color in daylight was a ruddy red and I couldn't miss the thick vein that ran down the side of it or the clear fluid that seeped from the tip.

"Fuck," I heard Walker mumble, just before he shifted me so I was on my back, my head on the pillows. He pushed the sheet back and climbed from the bed, not looking back. My mouth fell open as I watched him move across the room, rejecting me.

Luke took his place, kneeling on the edge and then moving on top of me. Braced on his forearms by my head, he cupped my face with his hands.

"I'll prepare for our departure." Walker's voice came from across the room and I heard clothes rustling, then his bare feet on the wood floor as he left the room.

I frowned, but Luke's thumb stroked the crease in my brow away. "Didn't I... please him?"

Luke sighed. "He will protect you, Celia, from anything that might harm you. But he also protects his heart."

I just stared at Luke as I considered his words. "I've known you both less than a day. Is his heart that much in jeopardy?"

Luke settled his hips between mine and his hard cock slipped over my folds, then sank into me.

"Fuck, yes."

I closed my eyes and tilted my head back and gave myself over to Luke. Yes, perhaps he was right. I'd never felt anything like this with John, and we'd been married five years. Perhaps the reason why I was so concerned that Walker left was because I worried for my own heart where he was concerned.

When Luke took hold of the back of my thigh and pushed my leg up and back so he could go deeper, all thought slipped from my mind.

A Wanton Woman

Luke

"What the fuck is wrong with you?" I asked Walker.

I'd come up behind him, put my hand on his shoulder and leaned in so that not everyone in the hotel lobby could hear my heated question. If anyone glanced at me, they could certainly tell I was bothered, but not as angry and frustrated as I truly felt. He'd walked out on Celia without a word or a backwards glance. He'd had his thumb on her ass, for fuck's sake, and then didn't even tend to her after.

I'd had to soothe her from not only Walker's departure, but embarrassment after having come while having her ass played with. She was definitely adventurous in bed, but she'd probably never considered ass play before. After I took her again—it was more gentle lovemaking than fucking—I'd shown her the smallest plug and let her hold it. We couldn't do more this morning since we had to leave town and make it up to Jasper by nightfall. When I told her we'd not use it until later, her relief was noticeable. She just wasn't ready for it yet. To say that we were overwhelming was most likely a gross understatement.

And yet, she'd stared at it with definite trepidation and doubt, but with some curiosity about it as well. That boded well for two dominant men who wished to take her at once. If only one of the dominant men wouldn't be such a pussy about all of this.

That was why I steered Walker out onto the street where we were less likely to be overheard. Where my shouting at him blended into the busy activity of the Denver street.

He let me do it, because while I was bigger, he certainly wouldn't let me—or anyone else—push him around if he didn't allow it.

Once we were away from the entrance, he spun about. His face was all hard lines as he put his hat on his head. None of the desire from earlier showed.

"I have no idea what you're talking about."

Two ladies walked by and Walker tipped his hat.

I waited until they were down the block before I responded. "You had a naked woman on top of you and you walked away."

Walker's lips thinned. "I had Celia naked and on top of me."

"What the hell's the difference?" I tried to keep my voice tempered. "She thinks she didn't please you."

"Fuck," Walker swore, scuffed his boot over the ground. He walked away, turned back, paced. His ragged breaths came out in white puffs before he came to stand before me again. It was a cold morning, especially in the building's shadow.

He had his issues that stemmed from Ruth dying. It had been horrible and I wouldn't wish an early, miserable death on anyone, but she wasn't the woman for Walker.

He didn't love her, although I doubted he'd admit that. She'd... intrigued a twenty-year-old and he'd made her his. But it hadn't been a true match. I wasn't sure if he was riddled with guilt more for being as instantly enthralled by Celia as I was or that he hadn't felt for his dead wife as he did for Celia. I could see his interest in our new bride and it wasn't just his cock that wanted her. He'd assumed he could go into this unorthodox marriage and just get a woman to warm his bed and to sate his needs, but he'd been wrong. Perhaps we both had.

Celia was so much more than we ever imagined.

"She pleased me," he said, finally.

"Too much," I guessed. "That's the problem, isn't it?"

He nodded once, curtly.

I leaned in, put my hand on his shoulder again. "If you want to get in her ass, then you need to get your head out of yours."

He grinned then and I knew I'd broken him from his reverie. But, I wasn't done.

"Ruth's gone, brother."

He sighed at my direct words. "I know, but I won't get trapped like that again."

"Trapped? You can walk away from Celia right now. Just keep on going," I advised. "The town can just find different men to inaugurate the new law. I'll take her back to Slate Springs as just mine."

"And let Thomkins laugh you out of office?" he asked. "He'll call you out, saying while you'll pass the law, you won't subscribe to it yourself."

Thomkins was an ass and he would do everything in his power to fuck with me. It had been that way since we were boys. Walker could shrug off his insults much easier than I ever could, it was just his way, but he wasn't mayor.

I watched as a stage nearly missed a man pulling a wagon of coal down the street.

"This fight isn't about me, or Thomkins, or the stupid law and you know it. I want her and I'm keeping her. If you're not in, no one will know differently, but you have to be the one to tell her."

While I'd rather share Celia with Walker—there was no question she was attuned and interested in both of us—I wasn't giving her up. She was mine. My brother just had to decide if she belonged to him, too. If not, he owed her at least the truth.

Walker shrugged off my hand. "And let you have her all to yourself? She's not Ruth. I know it. Fuck, when she got off the stage, it was like you'd punched me in the gut. She's ours, Luke. No question."

"I know what you mean."

I did. The connection, the sense of knowing, had been instantaneous. As soon as I saw her walking down the train platform toward us, I knew. I wanted her with a craving I couldn't explain, would never have imagined. I had to assume it was that potent for Walker as well. He wouldn't have walked out on her otherwise. He cared enough to leave. But, hopefully he was going to commit on an even deeper level. We were both invested now.

"And yet you walked away from her," I added.

"I walked away from how… intense this is."

I slapped him on the shoulder. "It's incredible, how perfect she is for us. But I'll keep her all to myself," I repeated. "No problem."

He huffed. "No fucking way."

I grinned then. It wasn't about the law. It was about us. We both wanted her and we were both going to keep her.

"When you left, I had her all to myself," I said, trying to rile him. It worked, because he narrowed his eyes and pointed a finger at me. I held my hands up in front of me. "You had her all alone when I went to The Lucky Swan."

One thing neither of us had considered during the three days waiting for Celia to arrive was how to prepare her to take both of us at the same time. It was the ultimate connection between us and we would not be denied. But, we would not hurt Celia either. Last night, when I'd fucked her, I realized we did not have any butt plugs to prepare her. And so I'd gone at dawn to one of the brothels in town, one that I'd frequented in the past. The owner knew me and had not only given me a small set of varying sizes of plugs, but congratulated me on my new bride.

While I didn't tell him she also belonged to Walker, the man wouldn't have cared. In his profession, he'd seen everything. Ménage was tame for him.

"Brother, it's not all about fucking," he countered, his words sharp.

I dropped my hands back to my sides, gave my brother a meaningful look. "Exactly."

And I'd caught him, right then. His eyes widened as realization set in. This marriage wasn't all about fucking, as he'd originally wanted. It was becoming acquainted with Celia, talking with her, discovering her interests, enjoying her, not just her body. She wasn't just a bride, a faceless woman coming from Texas to marry us.

Walker grunted and turned about, heading back into the hotel. I grinned, thinking about our bride. While Walker was considered the intense brother, the brooder, he'd held himself back. Cautious and wary. But now that he was resolved, I wondered if our new bride could handle the full effect of Walker Tate. It was going to be enjoyable to find out.

9

elia

"I do not need that many clothes," I told the men as they escorted me from a ladies' dress shop, Walker's arms laden with wrapped parcels. Luke refused to let me leave without donning a completely new outfit, from hat to boots. Now out on the street, I had to admit the clothing was quite warm against the biting wind.

During our foray inside the shop, Walker played the role of brother-in-law while Luke filled the role of my new husband. I understood all too well that marrying two men was against the law everywhere… everywhere but Slate Springs, Colorado. I did not want to draw attention to our unusual arrangement any more than the men did.

I was still coming to terms with what I'd done. Lord,

I'd spent a wild and carnal night—and morning—with both of them. Luke had fucked me and I'd orgasmed with wild abandon. Just this morning, Walker had even pressed the tip of his thumb into my bottom as Luke did magical things with his fingers in my pussy. And they'd done it together. Together! I'd had two men touching me.

The only time it seemed even the slightest bit similar to a conventional marriage was this morning when Luke had taken me while I lay on my back in bed.

But what was a conventional marriage? Had my marriage to John been conventional? Did other husbands take mistresses to their beds? I had to wonder if perhaps with Luke and Walker I was, in fact, quite lucky. I'd come three times. In five years, I'd had zero orgasms with John, so I knew what Luke, Walker and I shared was... unique.

The only similarity to what I'd done with John was the position. Earlier, Luke had been on top of me, just has John had always done. But with Luke, I'd been naked and eager and wet and he'd made me come. Again. He'd done it by sucking on one of my nipples as he brushed his fingers over my clit. John had never done either of those things. I'd never even gotten wet before.

I'd loved it all with Luke and Walker. Every bit of it. I just had to reconcile what I'd been raised to believe compared to what we were doing. I should be chaste and modest. I was not. I should be meek and submissive. I wasn't meek, but I seemed to be even more submissive than I ever thought. I'd loved the way the men dominated me. My mind, my body, my pleasure.

A Wanton Woman

But they hadn't pushed or demanded when they could have easily overpowered me. John had expected compliance, acquiescence to his husbandly needs. I'd never told him no, but I had to wonder if he would have taken me even if I'd denied him.

Walker and Luke had asked first, gained consent before they even kissed me. They were honorable, yet did an honorable man want to fuck my ass? And yet Walker seemed doubtful about something. Not me, but perhaps he had some issues as he'd been married before. Was that why he'd rejected me? Had it been too much to play with my ass? Was I too much?

I had to assume the answer was yes, but—

"You said yourself you have no winter clothing. Not even a coat or gloves. Your dresses are made of cotton, not wool. Even your stockings are for warm weather," Luke said. "While there are premade dresses at the shop in Slate Springs, it is better to be well supplied in advance of the long winter."

He tucked my hand into the crook of his arm as we walked down the street. My new coat, a lovely shade of blue, was thick and heavy. The kid gloves were lined with rabbit fur. But neither kept me as warm as the feel of Luke against my side, who seemed to be warm even in the coldest of weather. I assumed Walker was the same way, but he walked two steps behind us for propriety's sake.

"The livery is just a block away. Are you comfortable walking that far for us to get our horses?" Luke asked.

They'd told me we were to ride horses to Slate Springs, stopping overnight in a town called Georgetown on the way. I'd never heard of it, but both men assured me it would be a comfortable night. By the looks in their eyes, I assumed by comfortable they meant pleasurable. My pussy, which was a little sore and definitely tender, clenched at the idea of being between them again.

I was about to reply with a simple yes when I saw someone and I stopped as if my feet froze to the ground. My heart skipped a beat as I looked across the busy thoroughfare and saw Carl Norman. He was of average height with dark hair and equally dark eyes and could hide easily among the people walking along the city sidewalk. But it was his tanned skin that set him apart. While the sun was bright, overly so, in Colorado, no one walking past had skin the color of caramel, indicative of life in a warmer climate.

Luke didn't expect my stop and kept walking, tugging me along a step. Walker put his arms on my shoulders to keep from running into me.

"What is it, doll?" he asked, turning his head to where I was looking.

I stared across the street intently, Carl's eyes directly on mine. Oh God, he'd found me. All my fears hadn't been unwarranted. He was here watching me.

The corner of his mouth tipped up in a wicked smile. I gasped, then pinched my lips together. I hadn't told either man about Carl, that he wished me dead, even threatened to kill me for what I'd done to his brother. I'd sputtered to him when he'd cornered me in the alley that I'd done nothing. I hadn't pulled the trigger that killed two people. But Carl hadn't seen it that way and sought revenge. Sought revenge for the only witness to his brother's crime, who helped in his conviction, and ultimately, execution.

"Doll?" Walker repeated and I looked over my shoulder at him.

He looked across the street—God, I had to hope he hadn't noticed Carl—then looked down at me, studied my face.

My eyes darted to where Carl was, but he was gone. I looked up and down the sidewalk on the other side of the street, but he was nowhere to be seen.

Had he really been there? Had my mind played a trick on me? Was I so afraid of him following me that I was putting his face on strangers?

"What's the matter, Celia?" Luke asked. "You look as if you've seen a ghost."

Should I tell them? Should I let them know that their wife possibly had a crazy man after her? Would they even believe me? Would they change their minds about me, leaving me here in Denver? I'd rather be up in Slate Springs with a snowed-in pass, but that would only happen if they took me with them. I could tell them the truth, but later when I was sure Carl couldn't get to me.

A ghost? Yes, Carl Norman was a ghost and I had no idea how to make him go away.

I took a deep breath, let it out, then smiled, although

weakly. "Nothing. I thought I saw a familiar face, but it couldn't be. I know only you two here in Denver."

The men didn't seem so sure, continuing to appraise those on the sidewalk for a few more seconds.

"We should be going to make it to Jasper before dark?" I asked, hoping to prod them back into motion. Chills ran down my spine and it wasn't from the cold. The sooner we were out of Denver, the better.

Luke patted my hand in the crook of his elbow and we continued on. This time, Walker walked beside me so I was flanked by two imposing men. I was reassured by their size and protectiveness, but I doubted it could keep Carl away.

Walker

We rode into Jasper two hours after dark. Snow was falling so the route was bright, but I was ready to get out of the cold and into bed with our bride. She'd ridden on her own for most of the journey, but the last few miles she grew weary—not that she complained—and Luke coaxed her to ride with him and he held her on his lap and let her animal be tethered to mine. I was mighty jealous of him holding her, but I was also glad for the distance, for I would have interrogated her like a witness in court if she were in my lap. With my new resolve in our marriage, I was impatient to know about the man on the street. I was possessive and protective and I needed to know, but I had to wait. At least until we were all warm again and fed.

She'd known the man, whoever the fuck he was. We'd watched her alight the train in Denver and had kept her well occupied, so she hadn't seen him in town before. That meant she'd known him from before her arrival. Had he bothered her on the train or was he someone she knew from Texas? The way she'd reacted, equally stunned and afraid, was obvious to me, although she'd hidden it fairly well. That meant two things. She wasn't expecting to the see the man and she wanted to keep him a secret.

On the street, I'd glanced at Luke but he hadn't seen the man. His gaze had been focused on Celia. The stranger had disappeared quickly, as if, like Luke said, he'd been a ghost. He was no ghost. I'd seen the man's smirk, the roiling anger in his gaze, directed squarely on Celia, without question. Why? And who the hell was he?

We'd find out soon enough, because a man like that, with anger directed at my wife, needed to be stopped. While I'd been reluctant to take a bride—especially because of the new town law—I'd given in because I wasn't averse to the idea of a wife warming my bed again. But Luke had called me out when I climbed from the bed of a willing woman. From Celia. Hell, I'd been teaching her about ass play with my thumb. I was an asshole and an idiot, but I'd been fucking scared and panicked.

What other reason would a man climb from the bed he shared with a naked and well-sated woman?

I'd married Ruth when we were both so young. I'd thought it was love, but it had been youthful randiness on my part. She'd been beautiful and I'd wanted her in my bed. Ruth had wanted out of her zealous and strict parents' house. So I made her mine and when I got her just where I wanted her, beneath me, she'd been... disinterested. I'd wanted to show her the fun that could be had in lovemaking, even some more unusual aspects of the act, but she'd gotten all she wanted. Escape. It had turned into a stale and empty marriage, but I'd vowed never to go through that again. To be bound to a woman for life, to a woman who kept you from love.

And so when I agreed to the plural marriage with Luke, it had been easy. I'd planned to let Luke worry about keeping her happy while I just enjoyed the... perks of the union. But she'd stepped of that train and destroyed every wall, every defense I had. One small smile, one look of surprise when our touch brought her pleasure and I never had a chance against Celia. I walked away this morning, not because I didn't want her, but because I wanted her too much. I wouldn't do it again.

I was a stupid fuck and I was going to make it right. I was going to give her everything.

As for Celia, while she was so open and passionate when we touched her, she had to learn that we were her husbands and there would be no secrets elsewhere in our marriage. She would not keep things from us. We would protect her at all costs. Whoever that man was, he would not even look at her wrong again. But to help her, she needed to talk. I was willing to do whatever it took to get her to open up, even if that meant tossing her over my knee and spanking her ass until she shared.

10

alker

We rode up to our friend Lane Haskins' house; the downstairs windows glowed with soft lantern light. The man himself came out onto the porch and put his hat low on his head. Tucking up the collar of his coat, he came down the steps to meet us.

Luke handed Celia down from his lap and Lane was there to help her. Luke dismounted and stood beside her and introduced our bride.

Lane replied with a simple tip of his hat. "Ma'am."

Climbing from my horse, I joined them.

"Celia, this is Lane Haskins, an old friend," Luke said by way of introduction.

We'd known Lane for a decade. As a mine owner in

Jasper, he and Luke had the same profession, fell in with the same circles; he'd even housed Luke one winter when he'd been caught in Jasper after the pass closed. While his mine was smaller than Luke's, it was very prosperous. His house sat at the edge of town, the base of the mountains directly out his back door. Large for just a bachelor, he'd built it with a family in mind. He had yet to find the right woman. In the meantime, we stayed with him as we passed through, often bringing him supplies with us back from Denver. Not this trip.

Tonight, we only brought our bride.

"Stew's on the stove to stay warm."

Stew sounded perfect for my empty stomach.

"You won't join us?" I asked.

Lane shook his head. "I ate earlier, but wanted to meet your new bride before I left."

"You're not staying?" Celia asked.

"No, ma'am," he replied, offering her a smile. "It's best that newlyweds have time on their own. Don't concern yourself with me. I won't be cold tonight."

He would spend the night in his mistress's bed, no doubt, and would be quite warm.

It was too dark to see if Celia blushed with embarrassment, but I had to imagine her thoughts. Of course we would fuck her tonight. Hell, we'd fuck her every night... and morning.

"You must be chilled through. Head on inside and warm up," he told Celia.

She glanced at Luke, who nodded.

"Thank you," she replied. All three of us watched her go inside.

"I'll settle your horses for you, then be on my way."

"You've been generous enough. I've got them," Luke said, grabbing the reins and walking around the side of the house to the barn.

Lane slapped me on the back, knocking snow off my coat.

"She's lovely, Walker."

Only a few years older than both Luke and I, Lane was still in his prime and focused on his profession instead of a bride. The mine brought money, but it didn't put a woman in his bed or children in the nursery. So far, Lane hadn't minded.

I looked at the closed front door. "Sure is. We are... lucky."

"If that's the bride you get from mail order, maybe I should send in a letter."

Maybe he was more inclined to finding a woman than I thought. We'd been to the brothel in Jasper with him before and knew he had some unconventional needs. When we told him about our marriage, how we'd share a bride together, he hadn't flinched, perhaps been a little intrigued. He'd poured us some whiskey to toast our new bride and was almost as eager to meet her as we'd been.

I grinned then. "Perhaps you should. Thanks for the house tonight."

"I'll come back after breakfast tomorrow. Lil will keep me occupied until then." He winked.

"I hate to think I kicked you out of your own house," I said.

With one hand raised, he continued. "Please. I don't want to be the only one not having a woman warm my bed. Besides, you don't need me about if you only married yesterday."

"Probably for the best," I replied. "She's got some trouble following her, and I mean to get the story behind it from her."

"You mean from her behind," Lane countered.

I shrugged, some snow falling off my coat. "If that's what it takes to learn about the bastard who was eyeing her in Denver. She knows him, but isn't telling us. I'll spank her ass if need be. We're in charge of her safety now. I won't have her harmed."

"I thought you weren't too keen on this marriage."

I'd told him that on our way down to Denver last week. So much had changed in just a few days. So much had changed since Luke called me out on my stupidity. "That's true. I wasn't. But now, now I'm all in."

Lane's eyes widened. "Whoa," he said. "Fell hard, did you?"

I shook my head, laughed. "Hard. I'd heard of instant attraction, but this... hell, if it can happen to me, it can happen to you, so be careful."

Lane chuckled, definitely at my expense, and held up his hands. "I have been duly warned. It's good to see you invested in this, Walker."

"Ruth's been gone awhile now," I said, my smile

slipping. I felt lighter saying it aloud, to let my guilt of our failed marriage go. "It's finally time to move on."

Lane slapped me on the shoulder. "Good for you. If you need help with tracking down the trouble, let me know."

"Will do, and much obliged." I tipped my hat and Lane walked off toward town and his mistress.

I looked back at the front door again, thought of Celia. I had no idea what kind of trouble followed her, for Luke and I barely knew her. But with the attraction and desire, the absolute certainty that she was ours, it mattered not. The trouble that followed her was something we could resolve, could make go away. The rest, it would stay forever.

But she was holding back and I could not be in a marriage where my bride didn't give the marriage everything in her being. I would, for Celia. The secret would be revealed... tonight.

―――

Celia

Lane's house was impressive. While simple, it was large, larger than a bachelor could need. A stairwell was directly in front of the entry with a long hallway beside it. I could see the warm lantern glow toward the back and assumed the kitchen was there. The scents of bread and meat filled the house. I stripped off my coat as I peeked into the rooms to the left and right, but both were dark. Only one had a fire in the hearth, but it only gave off enough glow for me to see that it was an office of sorts; books lining the walls and a large desk in the center.

Hanging my coat by the door, I carried my hat and mittens to the kitchen. The room was lit by a large lantern above the well-worn table. A cast-iron stove was in the corner making the space quite warm. I sat on the small bench was beside it and removed my boots, placing them, along with my outerwear, beside the fire to dry.

Once done, I went to the stove and lifted the lid off a large pot set to the back of a cooking stove. The stew was filled with root vegetables and thick chunks of meat. My stomach growled, eager for some.

"Smells fantastic."

Walker's voice made me jump and I put the lid back on the pot.

He settled himself on the bench and did as I had, stripping off his boots. He'd foregone a necktie this morning and wore just a white shirt with his dungarees, his coat probably beside mine in the entry. "We'll eat in a little bit. First, we need to take care of your punishment."

While he was bent over and undoing his laces, his eyes were squarely on me. I frowned slightly.

"Punishment?" My mouth was dry and I licked my lips.

He stood and placed his boots beside mine. While the

kitchen had been so big just seconds ago, with Walker, it seemed as if the walls were closing in.

"For lying."

I picked up some folded napkins and walked around the table, ready to set it for the meal. "I haven't, I mean—"

"Who's the man, doll?" He crossed his arms over his chest.

I stopped at his words. So did my heart. Surely, he didn't know about Carl. He couldn't. "Man?"

"That's two."

"Two?" I squeaked.

"Two punishments."

"Walker, I don't—"

"Do you want to make it three?" he asked, arching a brow. With his arms crossed over his chest and the way he leaned against the wall, so patient and casual, it seemed he had all the time in the world.

I glanced at the back door, wondered where Luke was and if Lane would return.

"Tell me about the man on the street in Denver."

My shoulders slumped and I looked at the floor. "You saw him." I didn't state it as a question because he wouldn't have asked after him if he hadn't seen him.

"Who is he?"

"No one."

I didn't have time to make more than an odd gasp of surprise when I was pulled into Walker's arms and when he sat in one of the kitchen chairs, he settled me over his lap. My hands went to the wood floor for balance when he shifted me forward, my toes barely touching. It made my bottom stick straight up.

"Walker!" I cried. "What are you doing?"

I felt the hem of my dress slide up my legs, higher and higher until it bunched at my waist. I heard the crack of his palm on my bottom a moment before I felt it. Stiffening, I bucked on his lap.

"No!"

"You decide how long you're spanked, doll. Tell me about the man in Denver and we'll be done."

A sharp tug on my drawers and the string broke and Walker slid them down to my thighs. "I punish on the bare, doll."

Spank.

Spank.

Spank.

"I'm too old to be spanked!" I cried.

Walker didn't relent, spanking me consistently, his palm landing in different places on my bottom and the tops of my thighs. "You're too old for lies, as well."

I winced as he spanked where my bottom met my thighs. A tender spot, I cried out. He was not going to stop. I thought of Carl Norman and how he'd made my life hell in Texas and then he'd followed me. He wasn't going to go away. He was the one following me, pestering me, and I was the one being spanked. It was unfair. All of it. I cried then, for the pain was enough to push me over.

Tears coursed down my cheeks as Walker continued.

"What the hell?" Luke's voice boomed in the kitchen.

I felt the cold air come in behind him just before he shut the back door. He stomped his feet on the mat there and I could see his boots and lower legs from my upturned position.

Spank.

Spank.

"Celia's been a naughty girl and lying to us."

His tone held disappointment and that had my tears falling even faster.

"I'm sorry," I mumbled.

Slowly, Walker lifted me to my feet, holding onto my hips as I settled. With him sitting, we were the same height and I looked into his dark eyes. They held infinite amounts of patience, but also concern.

"We are very possessive and I will not have a man following you, watching you like that."

I wasn't going to be able to escape. The truth would have to come forth. There would be no more running, at least from my husbands.

"His name is Carl Norman."

Walker's hand came up and he wiped the tears from my cheeks with his thumb. "That wasn't so hard, was it? Why was he on the street in Denver watching you?"

The corner of his mouth tipped up.

Luke went around the table so he could see me. "Who the hell is Carl Norman? A lover?"

My gaze met and held Luke's. "No! Of course not. The idea of that man touching me makes my skin crawl."

Walker pulled me into him so I stood between his

parted knees. "Has he touched you before? Hurt you?" His voice was a dark growl.

I shook my head and bit my lip. "No. It's not like that."

"Explain. Now. Or you'll go over my knee," Luke warned.

"I told you my husband was shot. That he was in bed with his mistress. The woman's husband found them together and killed them both." I remembered what happened, shivered. "What I didn't tell you was that I saw the whole thing."

11

elia

Neither man spoke, but Walker squeezed my waist to urge me on.

I sniffed, then continued. "I'd come in while they were... fucking and went into the room next door. I peeked through the partially open doorway and watched them. I'd been stunned to see my husband be so vigorous, so wild in bed. He'd never been like that with me. But then the woman's husband came storming in the house, up the steps and shot them. He never knew I was there. As the only witness to the crime, it was my testimony that sealed his conviction. He was hung soon after."

"If he was hung, then who the hell followed you?" Luke asked.

I was learning he was not as patient as his brother.

"His brother. Carl Norman blames me for his brother's death. That I should have been a better wife and pleased John. If I'd done that, then he wouldn't have strayed."

"That's why you were skittish with us," Walker added.

I nodded and looked down at the floor. "I knew how John really liked to fuck and yet he only pushed up my nightgown and… and took me at night. It was quick and I didn't like it. There was no pleasure in it and when I didn't give him a child, he gave up entirely. But he did things with his mistress that… God, that I would have done with him. But I hadn't pleased him. There's something wrong with me because I didn't make him happy and he did stray."

"Stop." Walker's one word cut off my frustrated outpouring. "There is nothing wrong with you. If your husband wasn't already dead, I'd kill him myself for making you think this way."

"Damn straight. We'll talk about that later, trust me. For now, this Norman fucker. Why is he in Denver?"

I put my hand on Walker's shoulder, felt the hard plane of muscle beneath my fingers. "He threatened me. In Texas, he grabbed me about the throat, said he was going to kill me. He wanted revenge for what I did to his brother."

"And so you fled."

I nodded. "Yes. I had no money to leave on my own so I applied to be a mail order bride."

"And he followed you," Walker added.

"Yes. He's insane. I don't think he'd follow us up here to Jasper, but I have no idea. I was thrilled to hear that Slate Springs was snowed in and he couldn't get to me. I just want to get where he can't hurt me."

"We don't have to be in Slate Springs to keep you safe. He won't hurt you, doll. You don't have to worry about that. Why wouldn't you tell us this?"

I looked at both men. "Because I don't—didn't—know you and I wasn't sure if you'd agree with him, that I'd been the one to make John stray, to make him be killed."

"I should toss you back over my knee for that ridiculous idea."

My hands went to my bottom and I rubbed the smarting flesh. Both men chuckled.

"This problem, doll. This Carl Norman, he's our problem now. He wants to hurt our wife, we'll take care of it. All right?"

I looked at Walker with hope. I'd told them and they hadn't run away. I'd told them and they said they'd take care of Carl. Of me. I felt better, better than I had in as long as I could remember. I wasn't all alone.

I nodded, wiped another tear from my eye. "Yes."

"Good. Tell me something, doll. Did you like your spanking?" Walker asked.

"No!" I replied instantly. "Of course not."

He arched one dark brow. "Really? You said last night

you want to be tied up and taken. You want wild abandon."

I flushed, remembering I had said those exact words. I was impressed that Walker had listened so intently.

"Yes, but not like that."

Luke came around the table and Walker spun me about to face him, although he kept me in the circle of his legs. "Walker had you pinned down. You couldn't go anywhere. Could only submit to what he did. You kicked and bucked with wild abandon."

"Yes, but—"

He put a finger over my lips. "Are you wet, Celia?"

Oh God. His words, so carnal and dark, made me wet. Not that I wasn't already, I just hadn't noticed. Without my drawers, I felt the slick arousal on my pussy and thighs. I whimpered, but I shook my head.

"So if Walker slipped his hand over your pussy he wouldn't find it dripping wet?"

Walker bunched up the fabric of my dress and his fingers slid up my calf.

"What's going to happen, doll, if I find you all wet? Do you get another spanking for lying?"

"Your body never lies, Celia," Luke added.

He lifted his finger from my lips as Walker's hand moved higher. Higher still until his fingers were mere inches from discovering just how aroused I was.

"Yes, I'm wet. It made me wet," I admitted.

Walker's hand moved away, the dress falling back to

the floor. Luke stepped back and Walker released me from his hold.

"Good girl. I'm hungry. You?" Luke asked, turning to lift the lid from the pot on the stove.

I stood there, confused. They'd aroused me, made me ache for them, then walked away. I whimpered once again as I clenched my thighs together.

Walker stood, leaned down to whisper in my ear. "Punishment number two. Orgasm denial."

I whimpered, for I was ready to come.

"Later, doll. Later I'm going to fuck you. Hard. With wild abandon. I might even tie you up."

Luke ladled some stew in a bowl and held it out.

"Eat, doll. You're going to need your strength."

I didn't say much over dinner. How could I? I'd bared my one and only secret to them. They'd taken the dangerous fact that Carl was following me with an easygoing nature. What frustrated me was that they'd been much more upset that I'd lied to them. Clearly, they didn't like secrets. They didn't like not knowing of any kind of danger or problem. I couldn't blame them, but the fear of rejection had been too great of a risk, and resulted in a sound spanking.

But I hadn't been turned away. In fact, they wanted me more. Their care and concern for me was obvious. I highly doubted Walker took just anyone over his knee. The action was solely for me. While it had hurt, and the heat and sting of it lingered, he'd done it because he cared, because I had not been forthright with him. It made me feel... protected and oddly cherished. I was at odds with how that could be. He'd spanked me and yet I felt protected. I should feel embarrassed or appalled. I felt neither.

When they had me admit the truth, that it had been arousing as well, I'd felt overwhelmed and dominated. Hadn't that been what I'd wanted from them? That I'd asked for just the night before? They'd given me exactly what I'd wanted, what I'd needed, without my even realizing it.

But when I thought of being controlled, I had thought of how John had taken his mistress, tied to the bed. While eager, Luke had not been overly dominant the night before. Walker had yet to fuck me.

Now though, they waited downstairs, allowing me time to bathe. I even took a few minutes to look over my shoulder and stare at my pink bottom, to think about the spanking, how I'd responded to it, to them. They were overwhelming and I was able to catch my breath.

Not for long, as they were below. I had no choice but to join them. Not that I wanted to do anything else. I'd been wet and eager for them. I still was and this delay only made my need even greater. This delayed pleasure was a punishment I did not enjoy. I looked down, saw my nipples clearly against my nightgown. Hard and tight, they ached. So did my pussy, eager for their touch, for their cocks.

Barefooted, I went down the steps and into the library by the front door. The lanterns offered a soft glow and the heat from the fireplace beckoned. The men stood at my appearance. They'd unbuttoned the tops of their shirts, rolled up their sleeves to show off solid forearms. While I thought the room a comfortable temperature, they probably considered it too hot.

I was suddenly shy, even after everything they'd done to me, with me, in the past day.

"I thought we didn't purchase a nightgown," Walker said, his eyes raking over me from head to toe, but settling on my breasts. The rough timbre of his voice had my nipples tightening. The idea of being touched, being taken, by these two as they'd said was heady. It was also arousing, and definitely daunting.

"We didn't. That must be one she'd brought from Texas."

I ran my hands down my hips, drying my damp palms. Yes, it was just as I'd imagined. They didn't want me in a nightgown.

"You won't be wearing that to bed, doll," Walker said, only confirming my words.

"It's... cold out."

Luke stepped closer. "I assure you, you won't be cold between us."

No, I didn't think I would.

He stepped forward. "My brother was an idiot and didn't take you this morning. I did, and I want you again."

Taking my head in his hands, his gaze dropped to my mouth. I gasped when his lips met mine, for it was not a kiss. Not a kiss I knew. Warm lips touched mine, so soft and gentle I was confused, then he slid them back and forth over mine. His tongue flicked out to lick the corner of my mouth, then the other.

His mouth wasn't firm or his lips chilled. Nor was it chaste. This was hot and carnal and it was just a whisper of a kiss. A sound escaped, making Luke groan. It was then that the kiss changed. With my lips parted, his tongue licked into my mouth, tasting me, learning me. Tentatively, my tongue met his and it was like lightning, a heated spark that shot through me.

"Hey, I wanted her first," Walker said, his voice a rough growl.

Luke lifted his head long enough to snarl back, "Too bad."

I loved the idea that these brothers were fighting over me, that they both wanted me enough to argue. They were like two toddlers fighting over a toy. And that was me. They were going to play with me, taking turns, and perhaps as they'd told me this morning, together.

Luke's hand cupped my head, tilted my head so he could take the kiss deeper. I didn't object. I couldn't, nor did I want to. I wanted this kiss more than my next breath. It wasn't just a merging of mouths, but a merging of souls. It was as if he knew just what would make my skin tingle.

I felt other hands on me as Luke continued the kiss. I never wanted it to end and by the way he continued and continued, neither did he. Warm air caressed my calves as I felt fingertips slide up the side of my leg. It too, was soft and gentle and yet I gasped.

"Walker." I gasped his name, surprised by his boldness.

I turned my head in Luke's grasp and looked down. Walker's eyes were so dark, so filled with passion I caught my breath.

"Luke's got your mouth. I get the rest of you."

I studied him briefly, but Luke's moved to my ear and licked along the delicate shell, then nipped at the lobe. My eyes fell closed as I breathed, "Yes."

Walker made a rough sound of assent as his hands returned.

They weren't being rough at all. Domineering, yes, but I felt no fear, no worry that they would take and take. There was no take. They were giving to me. I was awash in sensation, especially when I felt Walker's fingers higher and higher on my thighs. I gasped again, but Luke didn't relent and turned my head back to claim my mouth again, to swallow all my sounds of surprise and desire.

Walker's hands stroked me, front, back, and then between. One hand moved to my bottom—still a little sore from the spanking—and cupped me as the other brushed over my curls and then in between. I couldn't split my attention between what Walker was doing with his hands and the way Luke was kissing me.

"She's dripping wet," Walker growled.

"You're always wet for us, aren't you?" Luke whispered against my mouth.

"Aren't you, doll?" Walker asked, raking his fingernails over the tender skin of my bottom, awakening the hint of pain from his earlier spanking. It focused my mind on him, on their questions.

Yes.

"I want," I breathed, my body heating. "I want to keep feeling like this."

The corner of Luke's mouth tipped up.

"Yes, ma'am." Just two little words that had me thinking that Luke and Walker were doing my bidding. They were touching me to make me feel good, not themselves. They were unselfishly giving me what I wanted. It was so unfathomable to me that I was left reeling. John would have never done something I wanted. It has always been about him. If I'd even mentioned wanting him to kiss me, or touch me, or fuck me, he'd think me wanton. And yet, he sought out a mistress who wanted just that.

John was gone, dead and buried and in my past. If Luke and Walker wanted to touch me and doing so made me feel... bliss, then so be it. I relaxed my shoulders as Walker's hands crept back between my thighs once again.

"That's it, doll, give over." When he pushed on the inside of one thigh with his palm, I moved my right foot. "Good girl, let me in."

12

elia

Their praise made me feel just as much as their kisses and touches. I was pleasing them and they were definitely pleasing me. When one of Walker's fingers circled my entrance and then dipped inside, I broke Luke's kiss and cried out. "Oh my God!"

Pleasure, so sharp and bright pulsed through my veins. It was just the tip of his finger stretching me open and I was lost. I couldn't wait for one of their cocks.

"She's tight," Walker said, moving just the slightest bit further into me.

Luke began kissing along my jaw, nipping the tender skin as he worked his way to my ear.

"I know. She's so snug, she fit my cock like a glove.

You're going to come for us," Luke added, biting my earlobe again. "We're going to get you nice and soft and wet so you're ready for our cocks."

I clenched down on Walker's finger and he retreated.

"No!" I cried, wanting him to continue.

"Don't worry, doll. I'm not going anywhere." Instead of one finger slipping back inside me, he worked two in, scissoring and turning them to stretch me open. I felt the burn of it, the tight fit and I hissed out a breath. Even after having Luke inside me twice, I was still unused to such attentions.

Luke returned his mouth to mine, kissing me as Walker gently worked my body. When he put his thumb over my clit and circled it, my legs almost gave out. A hand banded about my waist to hold me up. My eyes were closed and I didn't know whose it was. I didn't care, for I wanted what both of them were giving me. I felt surrounded and cherished, possessed and pleasured. I felt like I was the center of their world.

"I'm going to... I need, I can't—"

"Let go, doll," Walker murmured, never stopping his ministrations. "We've got you. We'll keep you safe."

The pleasure morphed into a swirling ball of heat that spread from between my legs outward. My fingers and toes tingled, color swirled behind my eyelids. It was as if the pleasure was lifting me up so high that there was nowhere to go but down.

I gripped Luke's forearms, my fingers digging into the hard muscles, holding on. I was coming apart, as if seams on my body began to unravel. With one surprising curl of Walker's fingers, the string was pulled and I came apart. I was flying, soaring, falling, but I didn't care.

I cried out against Luke's mouth, his kiss swallowing the sounds. My body shook, my hips shifting to ride Walker's fingers, to continue the pleasure he wrung from my body, to never let it end.

Before I returned to myself, I felt lifted, the room spinning and then the cushion of a couch at my back. The long hem of my nightgown was pushed up so it bunched about my waist. The warm air of the room cooled my skin from the bliss they'd wrung from my body. I should have been ashamed that my lower body was exposed to both of the men, but I had yet to recover. My skin was heated and coated in perspiration, my breath was ragged. Slowly, I opened my eyes to see Walker looming over me, the two fingers he'd had inside of me in his mouth. I realized that he was licking up my wetness, the desire from between my thighs that clung to his skin.

"You have to taste her, brother," Walker told Luke, who was kneeling on the floor beside the couch.

With deft hands, Luke lifted one of my legs up onto the back of the couch, the other he widened so my foot was on the floor, my knee bent. I was spread so wide he was able to move between them. Hands slid up my inner thighs to have his thumbs run over the crease between my leg and my pussy.

"Just look at her," Luke marveled. I tried to push my

legs together, but his hands held me apart. "No, sweetheart. Let us look at you. So pretty. Pink and plush. Walker had a taste. It's my turn."

"But—"

"If you don't like it, I'll stop." His warm breath fanned my tender skin.

I couldn't offer a retort, for he lowered his head then and ran the flat of his tongue over my most intimate flesh.

"Oh my God, what are you doing?" I pushed at his shoulders, but when his thumbs parted my folds and opened me wide for his tongue to lick and circle my entrance, then higher where Walker had circled his thumb, I grabbed onto his head and pulled him closer. "Yes, right there."

"I don't think she's ever had her pussy tasted before," Walker said. "Isn't that right, doll?"

I moaned then, my only response. Luke said he'd stop, but I didn't want him to. Ever. Luke's mouth was decadent and so very wicked. I could feel his hair brushing against my inner thighs, the whiskers on his jaw rasping my tender skin. I arched my hips, tilted my head back and stared vaguely up at the colorful shadows from the fireplace that danced across the ceiling.

"Luke's going to get that honey sweet taste of your pussy on his tongue, then he's going to make you come again. Then you'll be ready for our cocks."

Walker kept talking, a long string of dirty words that only heightened my arousal.

You're so beautiful. So perfect for us. I love the way you've got your legs spread so wide for Luke. I can still taste you on my tongue. I'm so hard for you.

Of course, with Luke's head between my thighs, the raspy feel of his whiskers on my sensitive skin had me close to the brink so quickly, but it was the dirty words that had me crying out.

"Do you want our cocks, doll?"

"God, yes."

Luke's mouth wasn't enough. Walker's fingers hadn't been enough. I wanted to be filled.

"She just got wetter," Luke said, his tongue lapping it all up. "She likes the idea."

Yes, I did like the idea very much.

"Come first. We're both big and we don't want to hurt you."

I shook my head, but I wasn't really sure what for any longer.

When Luke slipped two fingers into me as Walker had, curling them over a certain spot as his tongue flicked a very sensitive bundle of nerves, I came again. My body stiffened, every muscle tightening. I clenched down on Luke's fingers as my mouth opened wide, but no sound could escape. My fingers gripped his hair as I rocked my hips to make the feelings linger as long as possible. This time it wasn't as intense, the pleasure rolling over me like a thunderstorm across the prairie. It was still powerful and I was wilted and sated, overcome with pleasure. I was drenched in it.

With a gentle kiss to my inner thigh, Luke lifted his

head. "Like the sweetest candy," he said, wiping his wet mouth with the back of his hand.

Walker scooped me up and settled me onto his lap, wrapping his arms about me. My nightgown came down over my pussy, but my legs were still exposed. I pushed at it, trying to cover up my thighs, but I gave up. The steady beat of Walker's heart soothed my ragged emotions, calmed my breathing. His cock, hard and thick, was insistent against my hip, but he made no moves to do anything about it.

Luke stood and moved to the chair across from us, lowered himself down so his legs were stretched out before him. He was breathing raggedly, his cheeks flushed, his eyes narrowed and dark. A glistening hint of wetness still marked his chin and I knew that was from me. I should have been ashamed, but how could I? They'd made me feel so good.

After working one suspender over his shoulder, then the other, he undid the front of his pants. I could only watch as he gripped his cock and pulled it free. Then I couldn't look away.

"This is why we had to get you ready, sweetheart. To get you all slick and swollen, soft and open."

Luke's cock was thick and long with a wide crown at the top. A bulging vein ran down the length of it, the color a ruddy red. But as he slid his fist up the length of it and a bead of clear fluid seeped from the tip, it looked angry and needy. I realized then how much restraint he had. By the heavy press of Walker's cock, him as well.

My pussy clenched in anticipation, but I was thankful that I was, indeed, wet, for that would not fit without some assistance.

"Are you ready for Luke's cock, doll?" Walker whispered in my ear. "He's ready for you. Fuck, I am too, but I want to watch you take my brother for a ride first."

I rubbed my cheek over the feel of his suit jacket. "Ride?"

"Do you want his cock?" Walker asked.

I nodded against his chest.

Walker lifted me so I stood before him, his hands on my hips to keep me steady. "Then go straddle his thighs."

Luke watched me approach, his gaze narrowed, his jaw tense and leisurely stroked himself. Fluid continuously dripped from the slit and down over his fingers in a blatant sign of his need.

"Take off your nightgown." Luke's voice was dark and raw. While it was commanding, he wasn't trapping me, wasn't forcing me. It was my decision, my choice to follow his command.

His order sent a shiver through my body and I eagerly complied, lifting my nightgown up and over my head, letting it fall to the floor. I knew both of them could see me then, see how hard my nipples were, see my arousal slick and shiny on my thighs.

I put one knee on the seat cushion right by his hip, then placed a hand on his shoulder for balance as I moved the other.

As I hovered above him, Luke continued to work his

cock as he looked at me, at my breasts, which were right at eye level.

"Drop down, sweetheart."

I lowered myself; his blunt head nudged my pussy and I shifted my hips, letting the wet tip slip over my swollen folds and then settle against my wet entrance.

He kept a hand about his cock as his other went to my hip, guiding me to lower down. Slowly, ever so slowly he parted my folds and worked his way in, stretching and opening me up. My eyes flared wide as he went in. He felt bigger than the previous night, but perhaps it was the position.

I lifted up at the hint of discomfort, took a breath, then lowered again, this time dropping a little lower. I did that, up and down over and over until he filled me to the brim, his hand moving away. There was a slight nip of pain at being too full. My breath came in little pants as I shook my head, knowing I hadn't taken all of him.

"Luke, I... you're too big this way."

He shook his head, looked at me with hooded eyes.

"Shh, I've got you."

His hands on my hips, he tilted me back just a bit and that changed angle had him sliding in all the way. We both cried out at that. I slumped forward and rested my forehead against his, our breaths mingling as I adjusted to being so completely full. My inner walls clenched and pulsed around him, adjusting to his size as he remained still.

They'd been right, I'd needed the preparation, the

two orgasms to soften my body before I could accept such a thick and long cock. I couldn't remain still any longer and I began to lift and lower myself, all the pleasure and need returning in full force. I wanted to come again. The way Luke gripped my hips, he was just getting started.

13

Walker

My balls ached to fill her. Shit, just watching her ride Luke's cock—again—had me almost coming in my pants. Hell, it had been torture getting her pussy all slick and soft with my fingers and watching as Luke ate her out. It seemed I was a masochist. While I wanted to sink into her more than anything, I was getting off on seeing her with Luke.

I could only imagine the feel of her around Luke's cock and I had to wonder how he hadn't blown his load yet. Undoing my pants, I pulled out my cock, relieved to not be so confined and gave it a long hard stroke. Squeezing the base, I tried to stave off my own orgasm. I didn't want to come all over my fingers like a randy teenager, but instead deep inside of Celia. I wanted to feel Luke's seed easing my way, then to add mine to her greedy pussy, marking her both of ours once and for all.

Luke had pulled me out of my funk, had made me realize I'd been an asshole to Celia. Climbing out of bed when she'd been so generous and open, letting me play with her ass for the first time, had been downright cruel. I'd been in denial about how much she'd affected me. No longer. I was part of this marriage now. I was her husband and I was going to prove that to her for the rest of my life.

We were starting off slow, easing we could show her some more unusual aspects of fucking, as I knew now she'd be shy, but quite eager. While we'd primed her pussy for our cocks, we were also preparing her mind for more. Easing her into what it was really like between husbands and their wife. It could be anything we wanted. Tender or tawdry, tame or wild. Neither Luke nor I were mild lovers. We'd discover what she liked, where on her body made her moan, made her wet. Only then would she truly be ours, for she'd give us everything. It had started this morning when Luke had showed her one of the plugs he'd picked up at the brothel and when we made her come while playing with her ass.

She was shy and innocent about certain things, but eager too. Like now, riding Luke's cock, her breasts bouncing as she took what she wanted from him. She knew I was watching, knew I would be next.

If this was marriage, with her so eager and open, then I was going to be fine with the idea. I'd worried I'd be jealous of Luke, fucking what was also mine, but as I watched her ride him with abandon, I just got hotter, my cock thicker.

Luke sat up and nuzzled into the valley between her breasts, then sucked on one puckered tip as he lifted and lowered her, taking her as he wanted so he could come. It didn't take long. This time it would be fast, for we were both too eager for her. For me, I had the taste of her on my tongue and was just shy of coming.

Celia whimpered, then exhaled a breathy moan, her head falling back, eyes closed as she came. It was a gorgeous sight, her wild and lost to her body's pleasure. Luke thrust up into her one last time and shouted out his own release. He held her still as he came, as he kissed and sucked on her damp skin. I was eager to feel the same, to lose control deep inside her.

Luke caught his breath first, opened his eyes and looked over her shoulder at me. Gone were the lines of tension from his body, the clamped jaw. He was sated and replete and the smile that tugged at his mouth had me wanting to punch him in the face. While he'd come, my balls were aching with need. This was the third time he'd fucked her and I'd had yet to get inside her.

"Celia." His knuckles stroked down her cheek, getting her to open her eyes. "Look at Walker."

She glanced back at me, studied me, eyed my very angry cock.

"He needs you."

Damn right. I needed her with an urgency I hadn't felt

for a long, long time. Even then, it hadn't been like this. Ruth hadn't been blatant at all in her interest, letting me guide her gently through our lovemaking. Even then, she'd been reticent and had never given herself over to abandon. Celia, though, was so responsive, so eager. And so was I.

She moved to stand and Luke had to help her, both of them hissing as he pulled out of her. She turned to face me, Luke keeping a hand about her waist. She was three orgasms in and couldn't be too steady on her feet. Her cheeks were pink, a sheen of perspiration dotted her brow. Her eyes were glassy as she licked her dry lips. I couldn't help but groan, my cock pulsing, eager to feel a wet flick of that tongue.

Her hair was wild curls down her back and she had a flushed, very satisfied look on her face. No one would doubt she was a well-pleasured bride if they saw her now. Her nipples had softened and her breasts were plump and full, a perfect handful. A narrow waist flared into full hips. I knew that delightful bottom, every lush curve of it. As I watched her ride Luke, I saw that it was still pink from my spanking.

I'd thought her beautiful when she first walked toward us from the train, but now, with her mind quiet and her body relaxed, she was gorgeous. It wasn't her body that was drawing me to her—although it would most likely keep me constantly hard—but her spirit. It was light and after her orgasms, eager for more.

I crooked my finger and she came close, moving to

stand between my knees as she had in the kitchen earlier. There was no resisting her perfect breasts and I lifted my hands to cup them. I felt their soft weight, rubbed my thumbs over the tightening tips.

Her eyes fell closed as I tugged on them with two fingers. I took in her naked body. She was all soft womanly curves, full hips and a lush ass. At the juncture of her thighs I saw her pale curls glistening with her arousal and Luke's seed slipping down the inside of her creamy thighs.

As I moved my hands away, her eyes slowly opened. I tilted my head. "Kneel up on the couch and grab hold of the back."

I hadn't even realized I'd closed my knees, holding her in place. Once I released her, she moved, settling as I'd requested on the couch beside me. Her breasts swayed as she moved and my hands itched to cup them again.

Up on her knees, she faced away from us. Glancing over her shoulder, she looked to me, then Luke.

I stood and moved behind her, ran my hand down the long line of her spine, felt the heat from her skin, the softness of it, then curved around to cup her luscious ass.

"I'll never walk away again, doll."

I leaned in and kissed her bare shoulder, met her gaze. She nodded and I leaned back.

"You think you're not enough for us, doll? Luke's hard again."

Hooking her hip, I gently pulled her toward me so her

pussy was on display and at the perfect height to fuck her.

"Luke, where's that plug you got this morning?"

Luke grabbed the plug and a jar of lubricant from the side table. Knowing we'd use it on her, to prepare her for taking her together, he'd brought it into the parlor with him as we waited for her to finish her bath.

Unscrewing the lid, he dipped two fingers into the jar and coated the plug generously before handing it to me.

I held it up for Celia to see, glistening as it was in the firelight. "You liked it when I touched you earlier."

She looked at the plug, then at me. Bit her lip.

"You're going to like this."

Stepping closer, I slipped my fingers over her pussy, Luke's seed coating the tips of my fingers. I used it when I slid back and touched her puckered entrance. Coating it thoroughly, I gently circled it as I'd done earlier in the hotel room, then gently pushed inward, insistent yet patient.

"Breathe, doll. That's it. Good girl."

I didn't stop, didn't relent, but let her body soften and surrender. All at once, her untried hole flowered open to my finger and it slipped in.

She groaned and her head dropped between her arms, but she didn't move.

"Like that?" I asked.

"Walker, I—"

Nothing else came out as I slowly moved my finger in and out, just to the first knuckle, mimicking what my cock would eventually do, but deeper. Luke went around the couch to stand before her, to tilt her head up and kiss her.

He swallowed her moans and cries of pleasure as I continued to open her up.

She gasped when I pulled out, but I didn't leave her empty for long. Pressing the hard, slick plug against her, I carefully worked it into her.

Luke cupped her breasts, which hung down heavily. Taking hold of her nipples, he tugged on them, stretching them to the point where her face was strained. The combination of the nipple play and the plug widening her virgin asshole was too much for her. With my free hand, I brushed my fingers over her swollen clit and she came. I pushed the plug in all the way, watched as she closed about the narrow neck, the dark base a beautiful sight between her spread cheeks.

A wild scream escaped her lips and she tossed her head back, her hair long down her bare back. It was a beautiful sight, seeing her give over to the more decadent and dark aspects of fucking. And she loved it.

Uninhibited and perfect. She didn't hold anything back.

I couldn't wait a moment longer. I had to be inside her. I lined my cock up with her slick entrance. "I'll never tire of you. Of this," I murmured.

Slowly, I pushed in, her passage slick from Luke's seed, but the plug made her so very tight. Her languid state eased her body, allowed me entrance. She wanted this. The way her fingers turned white on the back of the couch, she needed it too.

Luke continued to play with her breasts as if he couldn't keep from touching her.

"Walker," she breathed, her head falling down between her arms once again, as if it were too much to hold it up. Her back arched and she pushed her ass back so that I filled her all the way.

"Have you ever fucked like this before?" I asked. My voice was gritty and rough as I moved in and out.

She shook her head, her hair falling free of the pins.

"Do you like this, doll? Do you like it from behind?" I stilled deep inside her, waiting. "Do you like a plug in your ass?"

"Yes. Walker, please move!" She clenched and squeezed, shifted her hips.

Sliding my hand down the length of her spine, I began to work the plug in and out of her, in a rhythm with my cock.

"Walker!" she cried, looking over her shoulder at me with widened eyes in surprise as her pussy squeezed my cock.

I grinned and moved once again. "Like that, do you?"

"I... I never—"

"You will, with us. This is what it will feel like when we fuck you at the same time, but we're bigger than the plug."

The idea of fucking her there, of being the first to do

so pushed me to the brink. There was no way to hold off my release.

"I'm going to come, doll. See what you've done to me. Made me like a randy kid."

I thrust once, twice, as I continued to play with the plug in her ass, then groaned as my seed emptied from my balls, coating her pussy, filling it so that it slipped out around my cock and down her thighs.

With my free hand—I didn't move my thumb from playing with her—I reached around and fingered her hard little clit. She was so close, so sensitive, it took only a few gentle caresses to make her come again. Her inner walls milked the last of my seed from me.

Leaning forward, I kissed down her back, tasting her salty sweat, feeling the frantic beat of her heart beneath my lips. She'd taken both of us so beautifully. Her inhibitions slipped to the floor like her nightgown and she'd given herself to us entirely. For that, I was in awe. Enthralled.

"We'll never get enough," I murmured, before I pulled out, picked her up and carried her up the stairs to bed.

14

elia

"Wake up, doll."

I snuggled into a hard body and didn't want to move. A hand stroked down my back.

"The snow's still coming down. We need to leave to make it to Slate Springs before the pass closes."

Walker's words had me opening my eyes. My head was on Luke's shoulder, my hand tossed over his waist. While he wasn't asleep, he remained still. The sky was just starting to brighten, but through the window I could see the thick flakes still falling. Heavier even than when we rode into town.

I glanced up at Walker, who wore pants and an unbuttoned shirt.

"It will close in the next few hours?" I asked, then cleared my throat. It was rough from sleep.

Luke shifted and sat up. I was amazed that I'd slept so well, and using him as a pillow. I'd always slept on my own side of the bed when married to John. I'd wanted my space. But with Luke and Walker, they didn't offer any to me. I had to settle myself right in beside them with their arms wrapped about me. For cold winter nights, I didn't mind at all. And what Walker had said was true. I didn't need a nightgown to stay warm when I had them.

"No, but it will be hard going. The snow will be very deep and difficult for the horses. I'd rather not get stuck, put us or the animals in danger."

The snow was deep enough in Jasper. I could only imagine what it would be like at the top of the mountain.

"All right," I said. Walker walked out of the room and down the stairs.

Luke climbed from the bed, naked and went in search of his pants. He had no modesty, just like his brother, which afforded me the opportunity to see him—all of him—in daylight. I glanced at his cock, which was quite erect, and wondered how that had fit in me. John was... oh damn. Enough about John.

Luke was really big and I remembered how he'd filled me right up. Too much, almost.

He grinned at me when he caught me looking.

"I love your curiosity, Celia. Unfortunately, I can't do anything about it until tonight when we get home. Then we can spend the winter snowed in and naked."

My pussy clenched. The idea definitely had some appeal.

Slate Springs was different than I expected, especially since we rode into town with the snow blowing sideways. There was no path, no route I could see as it was buried in snow and was relieved when both men knew where they were going. Any previous traveler's tracks—even from minutes before—had been wiped out by fresh snow. Even Luke's house was barely discernible in the snow. It was white and two-story with a porch, but I couldn't see much else and I had no interest in lingering outdoors to learn more.

Luke led me inside as Walker took the horses to the barn. It wasn't much warmer. Luke stomped the snow from his boots, then sat down on the bench by the door to remove them. "It's cold now, but I'll get the fires lit. Keep your coat on and soon enough, it'll be toasty in here."

He finished with his boots and hung his hat by the door as he tucked his gloves into his coat pocket. He walked toward the back of the house and I heard the grating sound of metal on metal, a cast-iron stove being opened and filled with wood.

As I undid my own boots, I studied Luke's house. It was comparable to Lane's in size, but Luke's was made of stone, the walls thick. It, too, was two stories and vast.

There was no question that Luke had money, for the furnishings were simple but well made. Rugs covered the wood floors and I had to imagine how good they would feel beneath bare feet in the winter.

Luke came back down the hall, gave me a wink, then went into the parlor to light a fire in the stone fireplace. It was cleaned out and stacked with wood, ready for a match. The tinder quickly lit and the room quickly warmed.

With the snow outside, the rooms were very bright.

"I have a housekeeper that comes several times a week to clean, but she has dinner ready for me at six each night. Sometimes she cooks here, other times she brings a portion for me from her home. Can you cook, Celia?"

We hadn't discussed household work and I had to admit, I hadn't thought much of it. "Oh, um. Yes. I can clean as well."

"I do not wish to put Mrs. Jacobs out of a job, so I would like to keep her on. Please don't think I doubt your abilities."

I offered him a smile. "That's quite nice of you. To keep Mrs. Jacobs employed, I mean. I'm sure we will get along fine."

"She will not be here this evening, so we will have to fend for ourselves."

Booted feet stomped toward the back of the house. "That will be Walker."

He took my hand in his and led me to the kitchen, the chill already gone from the room because of the stove.

"Until this weather lets up, we will not be seeing anyone from town," he said as he removed his boots.

Luke nodded. "Good. Then we can have our honeymoon without interruption. Let me light the rest of the fireplaces and get the house warm. Then we'll warm you."

The deep timbre of his voice had me thinking I didn't need my coat any longer.

Walker stripped his off and hung it by the door.

"She might run off, though, Luke."

"Oh?" he asked his brother.

Walker kept his eyes on me, but I frowned in confusion. I wasn't going anywhere in all that snow.

"We'll need to tie her up, I think."

My mouth fell open then, remembering I'd told him I wanted to be tied up and taken.

Luke grunted. "Mmm, yes. Once we know she'll not escape, I think we need to prepare her ass with the next plug."

I clenched down at the idea.

"We'll prepare her and fuck her. Again and again. This snow might not let up for days."

"Days," Luke confirmed.

They stepped toward me together, hands on the buttons of my coat, the hat on my head.

I had nowhere to go, nothing to do but be the center of their world. As they began to kiss down my neck, cup my breasts and whisper dirty words, I knew I didn't want to be anywhere else.

A Wanton Woman

Luke

Two days. We had Celia to ourselves for two perfect days. Two days we spent in my house with her, making her the center of our world. We slept, we fucked, we talked. We learned about each other. I knew now that she disliked onions and preferred to have socks on her feet when she slept. While she remained naked between us—we both enjoyed the feel of her bare body pressed against ours—her feet were in a pair of my thick socks.

There were no callers, no one interested in seeing the woman that I'd married, that I now shared with Walker. They would arrive soon though, for Walker had walked to his house to retrieve some of his clothes. We'd decided before we went to Denver that we would live in my house—our house now—and Walker had yet to move in fully. Come spring, we would sell his house. There was no doubt he'd be seen and everyone would know of our return. I guessed we had three hours before the most curious would come knocking.

While the journey over the pass had been treacherous, the snow heavy and the wind creating blizzard-like conditions, Slate Springs had escaped the brunt of it. Mountain weather was fickle and I was pleased to see only a few inches on the ground out the window. The morning sun was bright, making the snow we did have, glitter. Inside, the scent of coffee and fried potatoes filled the warm air. The cast-iron stove made the room quite warm and I enjoyed seeing Celia in just my shirt and socks.

"See the rope, sweetheart?"

She turned away from the stove and looked out the back window, squinting against the brightness.

"It's strung between the back porch to the barn. If it's snowing too hard to see the barn, you need to grab hold of it and use it as a guide, otherwise you might get lost."

"Lost?" She frowned. "It's only, what, fifty feet to the barn?"

"Mmm," I murmured, agreeing with her estimate. "About that. Last year, Mr. Demer went to feed his horses one night and they found him twenty feet from his back door the next morning. He'd walked outside, gotten turned around and couldn't find his way back. The snow was so heavy he couldn't even see the light from the kitchen."

Her eyes widened. "He died?"

I nodded. "You go to the barn in a storm, you grab hold of that line and don't let go. Just follow it either way and get into shelter. All right?"

"Yes, Luke."

"Good, because I can't spank your ass for not listening to me if you're dead."

The idea of Celia lost out in the elements had a chill run down my spine, even in the warm kitchen.

Walker came in then stomped his boots and shook off his coat.

"I checked on Mr. Bernard." When he leaned in to kiss Celia, he added for her benefit, "He's in the house next door." Next door was a few hundred feet away, but still the closest neighbor. "He's a widower and getting older now. We make sure he's got enough cut wood by the door to keep his fires lit. Other things." Walker glanced at me. "I expect we'll have visitors before too long."

I frowned, knowing that we'd have the entire town descending on us soon enough. Walker couldn't walk through town without being noticed and I knew everyone was eager to see who the mayor married under the new law. With his brother.

As she'd put it the first night in the Denver hotel room, she was the example and everyone would be looking at her differently. There would be those who judged, who criticized her and our marriage. They'd probably even think her a whore for bedding two men. But it was our job to shelter her from this, to protect her not only from her troubles, like the bastard Carl Norman, but from the troubles that fell on my shoulders, and Walker's too.

We just had to hope that the transition would be smooth. Not only was I the mayor, I had a mine to run and couldn't remain at home forever.

"Are you worried what people will think?" Celia asked, scooping fried potatoes into a bowl.

I saw the worry on her face.

"I worry what people will think about you," Walker said, taking the bowl from her and putting it on the table. "But we won't hide, doll. We won't hide what we share. I think it's pretty special, don't you?"

She blushed then, but nodded.

"He's not talking about how we both fuck you, sweetheart."

Walker grinned.

"We'll hide everything about how we share you," I added, my possessiveness making me almost growl. "That's private. No one sees you the way we do. No one."

"Especially like earlier when you had the plug in your ass."

She flushed an even brighter shade of red and turned back to the stove. I imagined the way the plug had parted her ass cheeks so prettily just a short time ago and I had to shift my cock in my pants. It had instantly become hard. Hell, I was always hard for her. She took the larger size well now, even fucking her with it deep inside her. It would be soon when we took her together, that we were truly joined as one.

"Luke is insatiable," Walker said, smiling and shaking his head. "I meant our marriage, doll, is special. What we have, this connection, is unique whether there are two grooms or one. I won't let anyone diminish that."

Celia's look went soft and her smile a bit wistful at his words. I agreed with Walker wholeheartedly.

"All right," she replied, then paused as she stared

blankly at the table. "Do you think... do you think Carl made it into town?"

When she turned her head to me, I saw the worry in her eyes.

"I can't say if the pass is closed now. The snow was bad up there when we came through, but it could have stopped."

I wanted to ease her fears, but couldn't.

"A stranger can't go unnoticed in a town of our size, doll. If he's here, we'll find him."

Walker walked by Celia and squeezed her shoulder.

"We'll find out if the pass is closed and if anyone's seen him from those who call today."

"You really think people are that interested in our marriage?" she wondered, sitting down at the table.

I glanced at Walker and he grinned.

"Definitely."

15

elia

We did have callers, just as the men had expected. First, Mr. Bernard from next door, who was in his sixties as Walker had said. While quite fit, his hands were gnarled from rheumatism and I imagined it was difficult for him to complete some tasks. I was glad to hear Walker had stopped to offer him some help. He'd been kind, yet curious about me, but had not stayed long. Then came the Johnsons, the Rands and then a small group from church. While no one said anything to me outright besides town news—the pass was indeed closed—I had no doubt when they walked back down the street, hats low on their heads against the cold weather, they whispered about me.

It was nothing I wasn't used to. The last few weeks I was in Texas, the whispers and looks had been unbearable. I'd had no one to shelter me as I did now. Both Luke and Walker remained with me the entire time, not leaving me alone once.

It was another couple who came up the walk that made Luke curse beneath his breath. I didn't know why he dreaded opening the door; I just sensed that he did.

Luke let them in, but with much less warmth than with the others. He was a small, rotund man of similar age to Luke and Walker. What hair he did have on his head—he was mostly bald—was fair. The way he stared at me with beady little eyes, suspiciously and with dislike, made me wary. While the others who had come to call had been curious, they'd also been kind. This man didn't seem to be kind at all. His wife was even smaller than he, her eyes downcast and her shoulders curled in.

"Thomkins, may we introduce you to our wife, Celia?"

"How do you do?" he replied. "My wife, Agnes."

Agnes offered me a peek at her eyes and a faint smile before she looked at the floor again. I thought her shy until her husband spoke. "Agnes has been curious how your marriage would be consummated."

The woman sucked in her breath and glanced at her husband, but remained silent. No, she wasn't shy. She was cowed, trained not to speak back to her husband, even if he spouted lies. I had no doubt it wasn't the meek woman who wanted to know about how Luke, Walker and I fucked. Looking at the very unappealing Mr. Thomkins, I had to wonder if they'd actually consummated their marriage.

"Thomkins," Luke warned.

"You know I didn't vote for the law," he began.

Walker sighed, but remained quiet.

"To see it now in effect will change the moral fiber of our town."

"Yes, we're aware that not everyone wanted the law," Luke replied. "But we are a democratic town, even though we are small. Everyone had a chance to speak and the council voted."

"You're aware of all this," Walker said. "You were at all the meetings."

"Yes, but what about church? The children?"

"We don't have any children. Yet," Luke added. "Give us longer than a week to get on that."

I blushed.

"I didn't mean your children. I meant the ones in town. What are they going to think?"

Walker came to stand behind me, one hand on my shoulder, the other on my hip. "That we love our wife, that we honor her, respect her and certainly don't shame her."

The last wasn't directed at me, but a barb for Mr. Thomkins. I didn't like him, not one bit. He'd made it very easy to feel that way. I felt sorry for Agnes. The poor woman had to live with the man.

"We won't stay and take up any of your time. We are having dinner with Reverend Carnes and his wife."

I didn't know the religious couple, but I doubted they would be overly welcoming either. I could imagine the four of them sitting there and gossiping about us over boiled potatoes and stewed meat.

"Then don't let us keep you." Luke went to the door and opened it, making it clear he was eager to have them go.

Thomkins stormed out and left his wife to follow. She offered me a small smile before stepping out onto the porch. Without anything to hold onto, she slipped and fell, landing on her bottom, but with her hand out to stop herself. She cried out in pain at the jarring drop.

Luke was crouched beside her as Mr. Thomkins returned up the snowy walkway with care.

"Agnes," he said, but it was more with frustration than upset.

She held her arm to her chest and her face was etched with pain. I knelt down before her and looked into her eyes. "Agnes, I'm a nurse. Can I look at your hand?"

Perhaps it was my soft tone or the fact that she was hurting so badly, but she held her arm away from her body. Her hand was curled and her little finger, while it should have been aligned with the others, stuck out to the side at an awkward angle. It was very broken.

"I'm sure you can see that your finger is broken."

"I'll take you to see Doctor Deeter," Mr. Thomkins said. Luke, Agnes and I all looked up at the man. He didn't even want to lower himself to help his wife.

"Celia is a nurse," Luke said.

Thomkins' eyebrows went up on his pasty face. "A woman to help Agnes? She's not having a baby. Her finger's broken."

"We can all see that, Thomkins," Walker snapped. "Let Celia help so Agnes doesn't have to be in pain longer than necessary."

Thomkins pursed her lips.

"How do I know you're really a nurse?" he asked me.

"You don't," I countered, then ignored him. Agnes eyed me, but warily. "I am a nurse and I can help you. Let's go back inside where it's warmer."

I looked to Luke over her shoulder and he nodded. He then deferred to Mr. Thomkins to assist his wife back in the house. Once she was settled on the couch, I sat beside her and carefully held her hand.

"Your finger is out of joint, not broken. We need to put it back into place."

"Will it hurt?" she asked, her voice meek and laced with pain.

Mr. Thomkins scoffed, but I ignored the tone.

"Yes," I told her. She deserved the truth. "Mr. Thomkins, will you allow your wife to have some whiskey?"

His eyes widened. Until now, I hadn't realized he had jowls, but they shook and had me noticing the way they wobbled. "Whiskey? Now see here—"

"She's not going to corrupt her to the devil's spirits, just get her numb from the pain," Walker told him.

"I do not need whiskey," Agnes replied. "I've delivered three children, one breech."

I blanched at the pain she'd gone through. I'd assisted in a number of childbirths to know what a woman went through to deliver a baby, but breech? I cringed and counted her lucky to have survived. Where were the children? With a nanny, grandmother? Or were they old enough to remain alone? Neither Walker nor Luke asked after them, so I had to assume they were fine. I was sure I'd meet them soon enough in a town this small and find out for myself.

"You're sure?"

She nodded, then met my eyes. She wasn't meek now. The pain was something she could control, that she had power over. Unlike her husband's usual overbearing demeanor, this was her choice.

"All right. I'm going to pull on your finger so that I can turn it, realign the bones and put it back into place."

I didn't delay, didn't give her a chance to change her mind. I didn't count. Just did as I said and quickly reset her finger. She hissed out her breath, but held herself still.

"All done." I let out a breath I'd been holding. "Luke?"

"Yes?" he replied instantly.

"I need some strips of cloth to bind her fingers together."

He turned and left the room.

Agnes was pale, her lips thinned with pain and sweat dotted her brow, but she was calmer.

"Your finger should be sore for a few days; keep it immobilized."

Luke returned and handed me a thin strip of white cotton. I smiled at him and went about gently wrapping it around her injured finger and the one next to it, tying them together.

"There." I offered her a small smile. "That should keep the finger still. Have your husband assist you while you are on icy ground to keep it from happening again."

While it sounded as if I were scolding her for going outside on her own, it was a direct barb at Mr. Thomkins for not being a gentleman.

Agnes stood and held her injured hand with the other in front of her chest. "Thank you, Celia. Welcome to town."

Thomkins made a funny sound in the back of his throat. "We are late for dinner."

With a backward glance, Agnes offered me a small smile as she was led from the house.

"At least he's got hold of her arm now," Walker said, watching them from the window.

I moved beside him to watch them and he put an arm about my waist. "That is not a nice man."

"That not nice man wants to be mayor," Walker countered.

I looked back at Luke, realized he was mayor to keep Mr. Thomkins out. "You have the job solely to keep him from the role?"

Luke shrugged.

"You were forced to marry me because of him?"

I couldn't help but feel panicked knowing the real reason for our union. He'd told me before, but being in Slate Springs made it so much more real.

"Yes," Luke replied honestly. He came up to stand on my other side, surrounded once again by my two men. "What Thomkins will never know is that I owe him a thanks."

I frowned, confused.

"I wouldn't have you otherwise."

"We," Walker clarified. "We wouldn't have you otherwise."

———

We woke up to snow. Lots of snow. Just like the blizzard at the top of the pass the other morning. It had been so cold and windy as we crossed and I'd been thankful for being in Walker's arms. I'd never seen a storm like it before. And now, another. I knew before the season was over, I'd be accustomed to such snow in Slate Springs. Fortunately, I was safely inside and once the banked fires were filled with wood again, the house would be quite warm. I stood at the window as I tugged on Walker's shirt. Neither man allowed me anything more than socks in bed, but when I did not have to dress fully, I enjoyed the comfortable feel of wearing their clothes. Their shirts smelled like them, their scents reminding me that I belonged to both of them. Ridiculous, yes, but it was comforting.

"Snow," Luke muttered from bed. He couldn't miss the sound of the wind or the whiteout.

"It's hauntingly beautiful," I replied, glancing over my shoulder at my men.

Luke was on one side, sprawled out on his stomach. An empty space was between them where I'd slept, and Walker was on the far end on his back, his arm over his head. Both men's bodies were covered to their waists and I reveled in the sight. Only I was the one to see them unkempt like this, to know the real men behind the gentlemanly facade. While they were gentlemen, they were also quite wild and wanton themselves.

"If we hadn't heard yesterday the pass was closed, I could confidently say it is now," Walker added, rubbing a hand over his face. The rasp of his morning whiskers was unmistakable.

Yes. How could anyone travel in this? If it was this blustery in town, much lower altitude than the pass, then I could only imagine the conditions at the top.

"I'll need to go and ensure everyone is following the snow plan." Luke climbed from bed and pulled clean clothes from his dresser.

"Snow plan?" I asked, running and hopping back into bed where I knew was still warm from Luke's body. I pulled the blankets up to my waist as he looked at me over his shoulder and grinned.

"Ensuring that everyone in town is safe, with

enough wood nearby to keep the house warm and don't have to wander out in the snow," Luke said. "Some elderly need food delivered. Even tending to animals."

"Like Mr. Bernard. Since we're the closest, I'll go over and check on him, make sure he has what he needs to make it through the storm," Walker added.

I liked the idea, thought it smart for neighbors to check on each other.

"How long will the storm last?"

Luke buttoned his shirt. "Couple hours, couple days. We never know."

"Miss Esther, she's eighty-four," Walker commented. "Her bones ache when a big storm's coming. She's the closest we've got to weather predictions around here."

I smiled at the idea of an old lady telling everyone bad weather was coming because her knees hurt. But, I'd heard others predict rain the same way in Texas, so I didn't doubt it.

"After some coffee, I'll get going. I should be back in a few hours." Luke came over and kissed me, then went downstairs.

Walker pulled me into his arms. "I'll take care of the horses, then go see to Mr. Bernard."

I shifted in his hold so I could look at him. "I'll see to the animals while you go next door."

"You're sure?" he asked.

"I know what I'm doing. I'll be fine."

He ran a finger over my nose. "I don't doubt your

abilities, doll. I do worry about you in the weather. This is new for you."

I laughed then. "Very new. I had no idea it could snow like this. I'll be fine. Luke told me about the rope to follow."

"Good. When we're all done with our work, we'll meet back here." He patted the bed. "Right here. I have plans for you."

My body warmed at his words, at the husky tone of his voice as he said the last.

"Oh?" I asked. "We could... we could do them now."

His finger slid down my neck and over the skin exposed by the partially buttoned shirt. "They involve both Luke and me... and that gorgeous ass of yours."

My heart skipped a beat. "You mean—"

"When we get back, we'll claim you, doll. Together. Then you'll be ours once and for all."

16

elia

With Luke already gone, I watched Walker out the window as he trudged toward Mr. Bernard's. It took less than a minute for him to disappear into the snow and wind. I didn't want either of them to leave, but that was a silly fantasy. We couldn't remain holed up in the house forever. Perhaps it was his dark promise of what we would do upon their return that had me longing for them. But chores needed to be done, there were neighbors to help. Until that was finished, I would have to wait, no matter how impatiently.

It took time to put on the boots, coat, mittens and hat, but knew I couldn't go outside without them, not even just the short distance to the barn. I took a deep breath and opened the back door, but the cold sucked it from my lungs. Narrowing my eyes against the blowing snow, I turned my back against the wind and pulled the door shut behind me.

I'd never felt such cold before. Even crossing over the pass hadn't been like this, for I'd had Walker at my back and a blanket sheltering me. My cheeks stung and my eyes teared. There was no reason to linger, so I carefully stepped down from the porch and looked across to the barn. I could see it easily and ran for it, my steps wobbly from the snow. By the time I pushed the barn door closed behind me, I was winded and my coat was covered in snow.

Stomping my boots, I brushed the snow from my shoulders and arms. The barn was cold, but without the wind, it seemed almost warm in comparison. The scent of hay and animal was heavy in the air. Taking off my gloves, I went to the first stall and rubbed the nose of Atlas, Luke's horse. As I murmured to him, he snorted, both our breaths coming out in puffs of white.

Footsteps on the hard-packed ground had me spinning about. For a split second, I thought it was Walker, having returned from Mr. Bernard's. But I hadn't heard the door open and he wouldn't have surprised me.

Before me stood Carl Norman. I gasped at the sight of him. He was no longer the confident, tidy man who'd harassed me in Texas. He wore a heavy winter coat, no gloves and a scarf wrapped around his head instead of a hat. He hadn't shaved in days, the dark hair of a new beard on his jaw. His cheeks were chapped and red, his eyes narrowed and wild. He had no snow on him, meaning he'd been in the barn. Had he been waiting for me? Had he sought shelter from the snow?

"I told you I'd come after you," he spit out. "I'd get you and make you pay."

I gulped down my fear. This was not a sane, rational man.

"My... my husband is inside. He'll be expecting me." I was surprised I was able to get the words out, my mouth numb. I was so afraid I felt my knees wobble. My heart was beating so hard it hurt to breathe.

Carl slowly shook his head. "I saw them leave. Yes, *them.* You're married to two men, giving yourself to them like a whore. No wonder your doctor husband bedded someone else."

When he'd confronted me in Texas, he'd said I'd been too frigid to please John. Now, he'd spun his reasoning all around. Clearly, he wasn't right in the head. And I was alone with him.

"What... what do you want?" I asked.

"To see justice served." He stepped over to the barn wall, grabbed a coil of rope off the peg. "You're going to hang, just like Neil."

He unwound the rope, let the length of it fall to the ground at his feet as he began to fashion a noose. I was going to die and Luke and Walker couldn't save me.

Walker

"The weather's pretty bad," Mr. Bernard said. With a cloth, he grabbed his coffeepot off his stove and poured two cups. Even with his rheumatism, his hands were still strong enough to grab it safely and I didn't offer my help. I'd carried several loads of wood from a lean-to by the barn and brought up by the back door. I also carried several loads to set by the stove in the kitchen. He wouldn't need to even go outside for more until tomorrow. I feared he might slip on the slick ground and with no one about to find him, he'd quickly die from exposure.

I glanced out the window toward the house. It wasn't Luke's house any longer, but *our* house. The house we shared with our wife, and hopefully soon, children. I caught sight of the lamp in the kitchen window, but then it was quickly obscured by the blowing snow. "Yes, I should get back so I'm not stuck here."

He handed me my cup with a knowing smile. "Why would you want to stay here with me when you've got a lovely wife waiting for you?"

Why indeed?

I grinned and spoke honestly. "It's different than I imagined."

"Sharing her with your brother? I'd imagine." He took a sip, then went to sit at his small table. "I remember when I married Lydia." His eyes focused on the cup in his hands, but I knew he was seeing the past. "A woman changes a man. Makes him want more. To be more. And when you have children..."

Mrs. Bernard passed on several years back and their children were full grown. One son lived in Jasper with a family of his own, the other settling in Denver. Neither had wanted to stay in Slate Springs, for there wasn't enough employment. In the summer months, Mr. Bernard traveled to visit, staying for a few weeks with each of them. But with the pass closed, he was cut off from them for the winter.

"I never wanted children before, but I want them with Celia."

"Then you better head home and get on that." Mr. Bernard winked at me and I felt my cheeks heat. "But you've got company staying. I'd think that would put a damper on things."

I frowned.

"Company?"

"That man. Your wife's friend."

I put my cup down with a thud, the coffee sloshing over the brim and onto my hand. A sick feeling spread through my gut. "Describe him."

His eyes widened and all humor slipped from his face at my tone. "A little shorter than you, dark hair. Tan."

"That's not a friend," I told him as I grabbed my coat, buttoned it. My heart was pounding and I tried to remain calm knowing who was at the house with Celia.

"Who is he then?" Mr. Bernard stood, went to grab his rifle he kept behind the door.

"Trouble from Texas."

He pushed the rifle in my hands. "I'm sorry, I didn't know. He stopped by this morning, first thing. He didn't even have a hat. I gave him one of my scarves to use."

I gave him a curt nod and opened the back door. "Not your fault. But I've got to go save my woman."

———

Celia

Carl fashioned a noose from the length of rope with a skill that made my skin crawl. Had he made one to hang someone before or had he practiced specifically for me?

"What if it had been Walker or Luke who came to tend the animals?" I wondered.

"I'd get to you," he replied. I had to imagine he'd kill them to get to me without even blinking.

"You'll be caught," I added.

He glanced up from his work for just a second. His eyes had a wild glint in them. "Doesn't matter. Justice will be served."

He was willing to die, accepted it even.

"You came all the way from Texas just to do this?"

"You *ruined* Neil!" he shouted. "Destroyed him."

"His wife did that all on her own," I countered.

He shook his head, finished with the noose.

"You couldn't satisfy your husband. He strayed to Neil's wife."

There was no explaining with him. It wasn't worth the effort. He'd come this far, a thousand miles to see me dead. Nothing I was going to say would stop him. And so I had to act. I glanced at the door, dashed for it. He grabbed my arm and spun me about to face him.

"Oh no," he said, his eyes wild, spit on his chin.

He pushed me back and I stumbled into the wall. The air left my lungs and I watched as he prowled closer, rope in hand. The length of it dragged on the ground behind him as the noose dangled. There were plenty of beams and rafters for him to accomplish the deed.

I slid along the wall, the rough wood at my back, away from him. I kicked and knocked over a shovel and I squatted down and picked it up. The wood handle was rough in my palms, the weight of it heavy. Lifting it, I held it out in front of me like a weapon. It was all I had. A shovel against a madman.

"Stay back," I said, my eyes narrowed, my breath coming out in little pants.

"I'm your judge and jury, Mrs. Lawrence. I find you guilty in the death of Neil Norman. You are sentenced to be hung by your neck until dead."

He stepped closer and reached for the shovel, but I pulled it back out of his reach. Grinning then, he stepped closer, his hands almost on me. This was it, my only chance. I swung the shovel toward him with all my might, striking him in the shoulder.

It knocked him to the side and he stumbled, fell down. The shock of it reverberated down the length of my arms, but I barely noticed. Dropping the shovel, I dashed for the door, pulled it open. It ripped from my fingers by the force of the wind and slammed against the wall. Tilting my head down, I ran out into the snow, squinted to see the house.

Nothing. The wind had gotten worse, the snow heavier. There was no path, my footsteps from minutes ago long gone. I knew the house was directly before me, but I couldn't see it. Luke had been right, a complete whiteout. I thought of the man he'd told me about, the one who'd died just outside his door. That wouldn't be me. It couldn't.

Looking back, I could barely make out the dark shape of the barn. I knew Carl was in there, that I hadn't hurt him too badly. Only stunned him. He'd follow, surely. He was crazy. Completely out of his mind and nothing was going to stop him. Knowing that, I wasn't going back there, even if it meant dying in the snow. I had to get to the house. I wouldn't be safe there either, but I wouldn't survive in the storm.

I couldn't walk to Mr. Bernard's where I knew Walker was. While I knew his house was to my left, I didn't know exactly where and it was just too far. I couldn't even go in a straight line without—

The rope! I looked up but didn't see it. Letting the

snow fall on my face, I walked left and right for the rope Luke had told me about, that I knew was there. It was my only guide to the house. It was just a few steps away and my heart leapt for joy at the sight of it. Reaching up, I grabbed it and ran for the house, stumbling in the snow a few times.

"Celia!"

Carl's voice was a bellow, even in the wind. He was coming after me and he was angry. Oh God, he was going to get me. I moved faster, all but running to get inside. I made it to the back door without getting lost, just as Luke had said. Glancing over my shoulder, I couldn't see Carl, but heard him. He called my name again and again, as if chanting it. I closed the door as quietly as I could, afraid if I slammed it he'd hear and follow the noise. There was no lock since Slate Springs was so safe, no way to keep him out.

God, were they wrong about that! A bubble of laughter threatened to escape as I looked about, searching for a place to hide. I ran for the stairs and saw out of the corner of my eye the rifle on pegs above the door. Sliding a chair close, I stepped up on it and grabbed the heavy weapon. I went up the stairs, struggling with lifting my skirt and holding the gun on the way. I ran into the extra bedroom and hid behind the dresser, slid down the wall so I was on the floor, knees up to my chest. With my back pressed against the wall, I tried to quiet my breathing so I could listen. If Carl searched hard enough, he'd find me, but at least now I was armed.

I heard the wind, the harsh whistling of it, the snow pelting the window. I heard my name once, then again, then nothing. I had no idea how long I sat there, knees up and gun ready, but I jumped when the front door opened and slammed against the wall.

"Celia!" Was that Walker?

"Celia!" he shouted again.

"Up here!" I cried. My heart pounded all over again as I struggled up off the floor. His feet were heavy on the steps as he ran up them.

"Celia!"

I ran out of the room and into the hall. Walker stood, a rifle of his own in his hands. He was covered in snow. His dark hair was completely white and as it melted, it dripped down his face. His breath was ragged and his knuckles were white as they clenched his gun. Eyes wild, they raked over me.

"Doll."

It was then that I wilted, that all the excess energy from what had happened bled away. My fingers went numb, my knees became weak and I slumped to the floor at his feet.

17

alker

I'd lost sight of the house twice on my way back. I'd tried to run, but the wind held me back. I tried not to veer at all, but when the house did come into view, I'd discovered I turned to the left slightly and was in the middle of the road. I slipped on the slick wood of the porch on my way to the door. All I could think about was getting to Celia, wondering what kind of danger she was in with that fucker Norman. To come this far to chase after a woman who had no part in his brother's crime, the man had to be insane. We'd promised to protect our wife from harm and yet it came right to our house. She had to defend herself from a madman. Alone.

Taking the rifle from her and leaving it on the floor

beside her, I wrapped my arm around Celia. She mumbled about Norman being outside, that he'd chased her but wasn't in the house.

I helped her to stand and took her to the kitchen where I watched out the back window for the fucker, rifle in hand. If he made it to the house, he was a dead man. If he was out in the snow, he was already a dead man. He could have returned to the barn for shelter, but I'd check later with Luke.

My brother returned a few minutes after I had, hearing about Norman's presence in town from Thomkins, of all people. "He mentioned that Celia's brother was here to visit." He'd stripped off his coat and dropped it to the floor, pulling Celia onto his lap, held her tightly. I doubted it was to offer her comfort, but to take it for himself to know that she was well and whole and safe. He breathed her in, just as I had when I held her in the upstairs hall.

"I asked if he was fucking with me and his eyes widened. Said he still didn't like me or what I was doing with the town, but he wouldn't bother Celia." Luke kissed the top of her head. "I guess you've got one admirer because of your help with Agnes."

Celia didn't respond, only rubbed her cheek against Luke's chest. Every line in her body was tense and I knew she wouldn't relax until we knew what happened to Norman. Neither would I. Neither would Luke.

We would not go to the barn and confront the man. Not in the storm, so we waited. I watched out the window and knew the minute the winds died. It took two hours and while the snow still fell, the barn slowly became visible. But we didn't need to come upon the outbuilding with rifles in hand as we were ready to do. Norman's body was a dark spot on the white ground, halfway to the house. Sprawled face up in the snow, it was obvious he was dead.

I turned, looked to Luke and tilted my head.

"What?" Celia said, popping up from Luke's lap like a child's jack-in-the-box.

"Don't look, doll." I stopped her with my hand on her shoulder. Her cheeks were pale, her dress rumpled and her hair half loose from its bun.

"He's dead, isn't he?" she asked, swallowed hard.

Luke walked past me to the window. "He won't be bothering you anymore."

She looked up at me, her green eyes pleading. "I have to see. I have to know he's gone for good."

I moved my hand and she went to stand beside Luke. A half a minute passed as she just looked at Norman.

"I did as you said, Luke. I grabbed hold of the rope and followed it to the house. I... I couldn't see a thing."

She put her hands over her mouth.

"At first, I got confused, couldn't see where I was going. I got lost. Then I remembered the rope and found it."

Luke pulled her into a hug.

"I don't think he knew about the rope and got turned around."

"I heard him calling for me, again and again, then nothing." I thought of him chasing Celia and clenched my fists.

I stared out at the body, partially covered in blown snow. "It looks like he wrapped a rope about his waist and ventured out. Not sure why he didn't just follow it back to the barn."

Celia shook her head. "He... he was going to hang me. Like what happened to his brother. It's the noose."

Holy fuck. I put the rifle down on the table and went out the back door. No coat. I didn't need one. My anger kept me warm. I trudged through the snow until I stood over the body of Carl Norman. In his hands was a rope with a fucking noose on the end, just as she'd said. I glanced back at the house, at Celia, at Luke standing right beside her.

It had been close. Too close. She could have easily died a gruesome, horrible death. Life was fragile. I'd learned that when Ruth died. I'd survived her death, the loss of her, our marriage. But it hadn't been anything like what I had with Celia. What I shared with Luke. If Celia died, I doubted I would survive it. I'd be a shell of a man, lost.

And so I walked away from Carl Norman, left him and his insane hatred behind and walked back toward the house. Toward my family. My life.

Luke

I saw the look in Walker's eyes as he made his way back to the house. Resolve. Determination. Love. He'd accepted Celia as his wife back in Denver, but perhaps he hadn't gotten it all sorted in his head until now. Until death almost took her from us.

He shut the door behind him and faced Celia. Lifting his hand, he cupped her jaw. "I love you."

Celia stepped into his arms hearing that, and I looked to my brother over her head. I saw the truth of the words in his eyes, heard it in those three words. He was with us in this. Completely. Utterly.

"I love both of you," Celia murmured against him.

Pride and love swelled my chest. Nothing mattered but our family. The three of us. Not Thomkins, not Norman. Nothing. This was what I'd hoped for from the marriage, but hadn't expected it. Then again, I hadn't expected Celia.

She reached out for me and I took her small hand in mine. Squeezed it. "This is crazy."

I smiled at down at her, shook my head. "Sometimes it just works. This love, sweetheart, I've said all along, is perfect."

It was. Absolutely perfect.

"I need you both," she replied, her voice soft. "Please."

"You've got us," I assured her.

"Not like that. I *need*," she repeated.

Walker pushed her back so he could look at her. "You don't have to beg, doll. We want you, too. Always. But we can't take you now. You've had a scare."

She shook her head. "We all have. It makes me want you more."

"We won't leave you," I told her.

While she was a grown woman, it would be a long time before either of us left her alone again. I knew how she felt. She wanted validation, to feel pleasure instead of pain or fear. "You want us to fuck you?"

"Yes," she replied.

"Are you sure?"

"Yes," she repeated. "I want you… together."

I arched a brow at her request. "Together?" She wanted us both, to fuck her at the same time. That meant I would claim her pussy, Walker her ass. "It's time?"

She nodded. "After what happened… what almost happened, I want to feel alive. Connected to both of you. I'm ready."

She was. We'd prepared her body well over the past few days until her body readily took the largest plug, but we weren't going to claim her like that until she truly wanted it. Now she did. Mind and body.

I took her hand and led her down the hall and up the stairs. Walker followed. We were ready to make her ours once and for all.

Celia

I wanted this. I *needed* this. I needed my men in every way possible. They'd been patient with me, preparing my body so I could take them both at the same time. It was the final act that would tie us together. I was the one to connect us, to make us complete.

But... there was something missing.

When Walker closed the bedroom door behind us, I knew I had to share my one last worry. The one thing that might tear us apart. "While we can come together like this, there's one thing that would show our love to the world."

"Oh?" Luke asked, unbuttoning his shirt.

I nodded, glanced at the floor. "A baby."

The thought of a child that had dark hair like Walker or fair curls like Luke made me long for one so desperately, but I resigned myself to the truth.

"You want a baby, doll?" Walker asked, coming up to me. I could feel his heat, breathe in his spicy scent.

"So very much. But... but I can't."

He tipped my chin up so I had to look him in the eye. "What do you mean, you can't?"

I licked my suddenly dry lips. "With John, it never happened. After five years."

"He was a doctor. Did he tell you it was impossible?" Luke asked.

I shook my head and Walker stepped back. "No, but he said it was my fault. I couldn't... I tried."

"We'll try some more," Luke added. "It's not like we haven't filled you full of our seed already. You could be pregnant now."

I put my hand on my flat belly. I shook my head, refusing to hope. "What if I can't?"

Would they think less of me? Tears welled in my eyes and Luke wiped them away. "Then you can't. We want you. We married you."

"But you want children. You said so when we first met in Denver."

Luke nodded gravely. "I want you more. I love you, sweetheart. Just the way you are."

Walker stepped up behind me so I was between them, just where they knew I liked to be. He leaned in, murmured in my ear. "After what just happened, we have everything we want, right here."

He kissed my neck and I tilted my head to give him better access. My eyes slipped closed and I felt hands on the buttons of my dress. I was quickly stripped bare and their hands were everywhere. Over my breasts, down the line of my spine, over the curve of my bottom, between my thighs. They touched me as if they couldn't get enough, as if they had to ensure every inch of me was unharmed.

My skin heated, my blood turned sluggish, my thoughts gone. I just felt. Breathed. Gave over to my men.

One set of hands cupped my breasts, tugged and

played with my nipples as another slid over my pussy, then delved deep. I rode the hand, rubbing my clit against it, needing the release. It didn't take long. I had been ready for them, eager to feel alive. I cried out my release, my body soft and so very wet for them.

Luke dropped to his knees and I looked down at him, curled my fingers in his blond hair. "Once more, Celia, then we'll fuck you."

Walker nipped at the spot where my shoulder met my neck. "Once more and we'll take you together."

Luke kept his eyes on me as he licked over my slick folds, then I couldn't watch any longer. My eyes fell closed as he flicked my clit with his tongue, then sucked on it. One finger slipped into me just the tiniest bit, stroked over the place that had my hips bucking, had me crying out his name. I tugged on his hair to pull him closer, to ensure that he wouldn't stop until I came again.

All the while, Walker played with my breasts and whispered dirty things in my ear. I couldn't hold back the pleasure, for the two of them combined were so aggressive in their attentions. My body had no choice to comply, to come so hard that I had no voice, that my body tightened and tensed between them.

I didn't even realize when I was lifted and carried to the bed. Luke shucked the remainder of his clothes and lay down. Walker helped me so that I straddled Luke, his cock directly beneath me. After two orgasms, I wasn't done. I wanted more. Needed it. And, I wanted to make them feel good, to make them feel the pleasure, the release that they'd given me. They needed it as much as I had. Still did.

Without delay, I put my hands on Luke's well-muscled chest and lowered myself onto him, his cock so big and thick it stretched me open, filled me to the brink. He hissed out a breath as I surrounded him, clenched my inner walls to hold him within.

"So good," he groaned. His hands went to my hips and he started to lift and lower me, move me as he needed. I heard Walker rustling about, then joining us on the bed. He was on his knees behind me and I felt him kiss his way down my spine as his hand cupped my bottom. His finger found my back entrance and played there. By now, I was accustomed to their touch, to a finger or a plug pressing into me, filling me up. I knew this time it would be different.

"Ready, doll?" Walker asked.

I nodded and looked over my shoulder. I saw his cock, slick with lubricant, hard and ready for me. My eyes fell closed as I relaxed, tried to breathe as he pressed the flared head to my virgin entrance. Luke stilled deep inside me, pulled me down for a kiss. My chest rested against his and I felt his warmth seep into my skin as Walker slowly pressed against my tight back entrance, slowly easing me open.

"Breathe, Celia. That's it. Good girl," Luke murmured.

I began to pant as Walker's pressure increased, as I began to open for his cock. Slowly, slowly he pressed against me; all of a sudden the ring of muscle gave way and the head slipped inside. Walker groaned and I clenched Luke's shoulders. My eyes widened at the feel of Walker inside me. I was so open, a little sore and very, very full.

Luke smiled at me, but I saw the line of tension in his face. I knew it cost him to remain still and if I felt how full it was to have both of them in me, I knew he could feel it as well.

Walker began to move then, very slowly, in and out. "That's it. So good, doll. I love to see your body take my cock. Deeper and deeper. Yes, like that. I'm all the way in."

He placed his hands on the bed beside me and I could feel his chest against my back, his hips pressed against my bottom. Both men were inside me, filling me completely.

"So perfect, Celia. You're the one who's brought us together, to make us a family," Luke said.

"We'll show you how perfect it can be." Walker's words were followed by him pulling almost all the way out of me, then sliding back in. I had no idea there was so much... feeling there. Too much, for I was ready to come again.

Luke pulled back and began to fuck me, alternating in and out with Walker.

"Oh God," I groaned. I was being fucked by both my husbands. Together. There was nothing between us. I connected them, made us one. I couldn't hold off my pleasure, couldn't keep anything back.

I cried out my release, my inner walls clenching and squeezing both their cocks, needing them as deep inside me as possible. They'd held back until now, carefully fucking me, but their baser needs took over. The need to fuck and fuck hard came to them, for they, too, wanted to come. They needed it, were driven by it. I needed this, their wild abandon, for it made me feel so powerful.

I was the one who made them this way. It was me who they wanted, my body that they needed, that they fucked. And when they came seconds later, they filled me with their seed, marked me. Claimed me. If there was no baby to come from this union, it would not be for lack of trying. They gave me hope, they gave me love. They gave me everything.

EPILOGUE

ight months later
Celia

"Is that my wife taking those stairs by herself?"

Walker's voice boomed through the house and I stopped halfway down the steps. I couldn't see my toes and my men were afraid I'd topple down and hurt myself. And the baby.

"You know what happens when you disobey, doll." Walker came up the steps to stand before me, a hand coming to rest on my very round belly.

"I get spanked?" I asked hopefully.

He grinned at my eagerness. "Needy, doll?"

I nodded and bit my lip. Yes, I was very needy. "I just wanted a glass of water."

"You just had to call for me. You know we don't want you to fall."

Both men had been very protective of me since we learned I was pregnant. It has only been a few weeks after the awful day when Carl had tried to kill me. It seemed that my first husband had been sterile. I was not barren in the slightest and my husbands were very virile. They were quite proud of the fact and based on the size of my belly, I had to question twins.

We didn't, however, question my constant need for their cocks. I'd become voracious in my pregnancy and having two husbands certainly worked to my advantage to assuage this need.

Walker took my hand and led me back up the steps. "Luke!" he called.

"Yes?" He responded from somewhere downstairs.

"Our wife, she needs us again."

Walker escorted me to the bed, lifted my nightgown up and over my head to reveal my nakedness. The windows were open to the summer air. It wasn't hot like Texas, but perfect. Even so, my sensitive nipples tightened in the cool air.

I'd worried if they would like my altered shape, but they reveled in my additional curves and never ceased to tell me. "Up on your hands and knees, doll. If you want a spanking and a good fucking, then get into position."

Eager, yet with a slow pace, I crawled up onto the bed and grabbed hold of the headboard. Since I couldn't be on my stomach any longer—I hadn't seen my feet in a few months—my men had been creative in how to take me.

"Is your pussy needy?" Luke asked from the doorway.

"Yes, Luke," I breathed, taking in my handsome husband.

When Walker knelt on the bed behind me and gave my bottom a sharp spanking, I cried out. "Yes! More."

Luke closed the door behind him and came around to the other side of the bed, knelt beside me, cupped one of my full, tender breasts. We'd discovered that I truly did like fucking a little rough and full of wild abandon. I got wet from a spanking or being tied up. I just liked my men in control.

"We've got you, sweetheart. Always. You'll always be between us just like this. You're going to give us a beautiful baby and we'll give you everything you need."

They saw to me then and I gave over to their touch, to being the center of their world. The men never let me forget.

WANT MORE?

———

Read an excerpt from A Wild Woman, Mail Order Bride of Slate Springs - Book 2

———

EXCERPT - A WILD WOMAN

Piper Dare

My head lolled when the stage lurched in a particularly large rut and I woke with a start. Drool dotted the corner of my mouth and I wiped it with my fingers. I glanced up to make sure the woman across from me hadn't seen my less than ladylike spit, but she—thankfully—was asleep, her head tilted back so her chin was angled up toward me. It was quite warm and even with the flaps over the windows open, there wasn't much breeze. I tugged at my bodice, the fabric damp and clinging to my skin. I had a mighty thirst and longed for a cool glass of lemonade. I blinked once, then rubbed my eyes. Time passed slowly in the stage and I had no idea how long I had rested. Even with a crook in my neck and a sore back... and bottom from the hard and uncomfortable seat, it couldn't have

Excerpt - A Wild Woman

been for long. Based on the position of the sun in the sky, it should only be another hour or two before the next stop. My last stop.

I'd almost run out of coin and the stage would take me no further than the next town without expecting more. I was glad to be away from Wichita, yet knew my brothers could easily track me; they just had to follow the stage's path. I'd been gone six days already and had to hope the note I'd left, telling them I was staying in town with my friend, Rachel, had stalled their search by a few days. By now, though, they had to know I'd disappeared. They would come for me, I was sure of it. With five older brothers, none married, no one else was going to cook and clean for them. No women seemed eager to marry the lot of them, so they needed someone to take care of them. Meaning me. I had no intention of being their slave. I couldn't find a husband of my own if I was too busy taking care of them.

Besides all that, they were ridiculously overprotective. They chased off every possible suitor with their dark stares, cautionary words and loaded rifles. They didn't hesitate to shoot at the man's feet to get him moving if he lingered near me too long.

I was twenty-two years old and on the verge of being an old maid, but they only saw me as their baby sister. I hadn't even been kissed! Hell, they hadn't let a man get close enough to shake my hand, let alone put his lips on mine.

While none of them were cruel and I knew they loved

me, perhaps they loved me a little too much. I didn't need to be sheltered and I certainly didn't need to become their maid. They needed wives of their own and I needed a life of my own. A husband.

And so I'd secretly saved up some of the house money, slowly but surely, until I had enough for a ticket on the stage. Unfortunately, it would only take me so far... and that distance seemed to be the next town.

I peeked out the window; prairie as far as the eye could see. I was used to that living on the outskirts of Wichita, but there wasn't a town of its size nearby now. There was nothing. Would I be able to find work? I could find a job as a maid, a housekeeper, a cook, even a laundress. I'd done it all and was not averse to hard work, if it could be found. I'd rather find a saloon and a game of cards, but I couldn't be choosy if I was broke. At least it was warm this time of year; I could sleep beneath the stars if I needed to. I'd done that before, too.

The stage jolted and I put my hand out instinctively so as not to bump into the wall. The other woman's head lolled to the side and I was impressed with her ability to sleep so deeply. She'd introduced herself to me when she'd joined me in Dodge City. Miss Patricia Strong, a mail order bride. She was going to a small town in Colorado, Slate Springs was the name, to meet a new husband. A husband that she'd been matched to through an agency. I couldn't imagine marrying a stranger, but I knew women struggled in ways men didn't. She was so lovely with her pale hair and eyes and kind demeanor, I

Excerpt - A Wild Woman

had to imagine beaux swarmed about her like bees to a flower. If she had to volunteer to be a mail order bride, what hope was there for me?

I had red hair. Red! It was like fire and everyone said I had the personality to match. I'd been impressed with Patricia's ability to take charge of her life, to decide on a path and follow through. To find a husband when one wouldn't come calling. Or in my case, couldn't. Not with a brother blockade in the way.

The stage jolted again. I rolled my eyes and sighed, wishing to yell at the stage driver, although it wasn't his fault there were deep ruts in the path. Out of the corner of my eye, I saw Patricia slide sideways, tipping forward as if she were going to tumble forward. Reaching out, I grabbed her shoulder before she hit the dusty wood floor.

"Patricia!" I cried, pushing her back upright, her head settling into the corner awkwardly.

The woman didn't wake, didn't put her arms out to push herself up. Didn't even stir.

I stood, putting one hand on the wall for balance, and leaned over her. I knew the journey was wearying, but this was a sound sleep. Too sound.

It was then that I realized she wasn't sleeping. She was dead.

"Stop the stage!" I shouted, pushing off the wall away from her. "Stop the damn stage!"

Dropping back into the bench seat across from Patricia, I pounded on the wall that separated me from the driver as I stared wide-eyed, mouth open.

Excerpt - A Wild Woman

She was dead.

I knew it wasn't ladylike to swear, but if there was ever a moment to do so, this was it. "Holy fucking hell. Shit on a stick, this is bad." I kept mumbling every swear word I ever heard my brothers use as I just looked at Patricia.

She was pale, white even. Her lips were no longer pink, but an odd shade of gray, as if all of her color had leached from her. Her body was limp and jostled as the stage came to a halt. I had to put my hand out to keep her from falling on me once again. Cringing, I pushed her back upright.

Once we came to a standstill, I opened the door and jumped down, struggling with my skirts before tripping and landing on my knees in the dirt.

"What the tarnation, woman?" The stage driver hopped from his raised seat and spat tobacco juice into the tall grass, hands on hips.

Spinning about, I pointed with a shaky finger at the open door and Patricia's prostrate body.

Swallowing heavily, I took a deep breath. The sun beat down upon us and I felt perspiration dot my brow. "She's dead."

The driver looked at me as if I was joking with him. When I didn't get up off the ground, he walked to the open door and peeked inside.

"Fuck," he swore, then looked up at the sky. It was as if he were silently asking God why the woman was dead, in his stage. "She was fine two hours ago. What the hell happened to her?"

Excerpt - A Wild Woman

He took off his hat, ran his fingers through his sweaty hair. He was in his forties with a graying beard and was missing a few teeth. He was travel worn, body and soul, and I had to assume Patricia was not his first dead body.

It was mine, however, and I was glad for the hard ground beneath me. I'd never been considered missish, but I'd never had someone die right in front of me before, especially someone as young as Patricia.

As I shook my head, I replied, "How the hell should I know?"

The driver's eyebrow winged up at my use of the word "hell." That was nothing. Being raised by brothers had taught me quite a few unladylike things.

"I have no idea," I added, finally answering his question. "We were asleep and she just didn't wake up."

He frowned at me, spit on the ground again. "People don't just *not* wake up. Not at her age. Hell, she can't be more than twenty." He waved his hands in the air as if that would help, as if arguing with me would change anything. It didn't matter *how* she died. It wasn't as if we could fix it, or her.

"Well, she certainly isn't going to wake up," I countered. The wind blowing over the grass, the chirping of the grasshoppers seemed so normal, as if we didn't have to figure out what to do with a dead woman.

"Fine, let's go then." He reached into the stage.

"What? You're just going to leave her out here?" My voice went loud and shrill, my queasiness growing at the casual attitude this man had for the dead.

Excerpt - A Wild Woman

He sighed, shook his head as he walked away from the stage.

"Sitting here gabbing isn't making her any fresher," he grumbled. "You'll have to stay in the stage with her until we get to the next town, where you're getting off."

He glanced at the dead woman again, then at the vast prairie, probably ready to change his mind.

"While I have no interest in spending one more second in the stage with a dead body, it just isn't honorable or the least bit Christian just to leave her out to rot."

"Hope there's an undertaker at the next town, too," he grumbled, spitting in the grass.

Poor woman. Patricia was—had been—so brave. As she'd shared her story, I'd actually been a little jealous. Knowing a man was waiting at her final destination was quite enviable. Someone who wanted her enough to submit an advertisement and pay her way. Someone who was actually eager for her.

And then there was me, homeless and destitute as soon as we arrived at the next stop. No man. No husband. No—

An idea formed in my head, making my heart skip a beat. Patricia had a man waiting for her. A husband. Someone who wanted a wife. He didn't care particularly who since he'd chosen a mail order bride. A stranger. *I* could be the mail order bride. I could take Patricia's place.

It could work. *Couldn't it?* Was it right to take advantage of a dead woman? I stood on shaky legs and

Excerpt - A Wild Woman

glanced at Patricia's dead body, then away. She was no longer of this world and wouldn't care. She wouldn't blame me. Hell and tarnation, women had to take advantages that were given to them.

"All right. I'll stay in the back with her," I told the driver.

I tilted my chin up, met the man's sharp gaze as I walked over to the stage, peeked in, then reached for my small bag. "But you'll take me to where Miss Strong was headed."

"Take you..." He shoved his hat back on his head, spit into the grass again. "I see what you're about."

"Oh?" I asked. "And what's that?"

"You're going to take her place."

I slid my gun from my bag, aimed it at him. He slowly raised his hands.

"And you were going to leave a passenger out on the prairie for the wolves," I argued.

"Now there's no need for a gun." He eyed me. Not fearfully, but suspiciously. "What kind of lady are you?"

"The kind of lady who has five older brothers. A gun adds a certain level of... assurance that you'll do the right thing by me and take me to Pueblo and the man she was to marry."

"And the right thing is to let you become a stranger's wife?"

Obviously, he knew more about Patricia than he did me.

"The man waiting in Pueblo requested a woman, not

specifically Miss Strong. Listen, Mr.... um, driver." I had no idea of his name. "My brothers taught me a few things besides shooting." I gave a slight shrug, but the gun didn't even quiver. "They taught me to take an opportunity when it falls in my lap."

Even when it was a dead body.

Did I want to marry a man I'd never met? Patricia was going to do it. Why couldn't I? It's what I wanted, a man of my own, children someday. But I knew nothing of him. What if he was old or had seven children already? What if he was mean? A drunk? Well, I could just shoot him. It would serve him right.

The driver thought for a moment, scratched the back of his neck, then slowly he shook his head. "Don't matter to me one way or another. Her way's been paid and I'd rather not have to explain to the man when I get to Pueblo that his wife just up and died."

I lowered the gun then. "So we'll be doing each other a favor."

He walked toward the front of the stage, hoisted himself up. He looked down at me before he climbed up onto the high bench, then pointed into the stage. "We're leaving Miss Strong's body at the next stop and we're not waiting for her burial. I have a schedule to keep and you have a man to meet."

While seeing the woman properly buried was the right thing to do, I knew I couldn't argue. I was gaining a husband.

GET A FREE BOOK!

JOIN MY MAILING LIST TO BE THE FIRST TO KNOW OF NEW RELEASES, FREE BOOKS, SPECIAL PRICES AND OTHER AUTHOR GIVEAWAYS.

http://freeromanceread.com

ABOUT THE AUTHOR

Vanessa Vale is the *USA Today* Bestselling author of over 40 books, sexy romance novels, including her popular Bridgewater historical romance series and hot contemporary romances featuring unapologetic bad boys who don't just fall in love, they fall hard. When she's not writing, Vanessa savors the insanity of raising two boys, is figuring out how many meals she can make with a pressure cooker, and teaches a pretty mean karate class. While she's not as skilled at social media as her kids, she loves to interact with readers.

Instagram

www.vanessavaleauthor.com

ALSO BY VANESSA VALE

Bridgewater County Series

Ride Me Dirty

Claim Me Hard

Take Me Fast

Hold Me Close

Make Me Yours

Kiss Me Crazy

Mail Order Bride of Slate Springs Series

A Wanton Woman

A Wild Woman

A Wicked Woman

Bridgewater Ménage Series

Their Runaway Bride

Their Kidnapped Bride

Their Wayward Bride

Their Captivated Bride

Their Treasured Bride

Their Christmas Bride

Their Reluctant Bride

Their Stolen Bride

Their Brazen Bride

Their Bridgewater Brides- Books 1-3 Boxed Set

Outlaw Brides Series

Flirting With The Law

MMA Fighter Romance Series

Fight For Her

Wildflower Bride Series

Rose

Hyacinth

Dahlia

Daisy

Lily

Montana Men Series

The Lawman

The Cowboy

The Outlaw

Montana Maidens Series

Claiming Catherine

Taming Tessa

Dominating Devney

Submitting Sarah

Standalone Reads

Western Widows

Sweet Justice

[Mine To Take](#)

[Relentless](#)

[Sleepless Night](#)

[Man Candy - A Coloring Book](#)

[The Alien's Mate: Cowgirls and Aliens](#)

Manufactured by Amazon.ca
Acheson, AB